HOUR OF THE CRAB

ALSO BY PATRICIA ROBERTSON

The Goldfish Dancer

City of Orphans

For Heidi ~ with a big thank you for inviting me to the book club!

Patricia R
Aug 2021

PATRICIA ROBERTSON

HOUR
OF
THE
CRAB

stories

GOOSE LANE EDITIONS

Edited by Bethany Gibson.
Cover and page design by Julie Scriver.
Cover image *Der Marsch* by Jr Korpa, unsplash.com.
Printed in Canada by Friesens.
10 9 8 7 6 5 4 3 2 1

Library and Archives Canada Cataloguing in Publication

Title: Hour of the crab / Patricia Robertson.
Names: Robertson, Patricia, 1948- author.
Description: Short stories.
Identifiers: Canadiana (print) 20200210297 | Canadiana (ebook) 20200210300 |
ISBN 9781773101606 (softcover) | ISBN 9781773101613 (EPUB) |
ISBN 9781773101620 (Kindle)
Classification: LCC PS8585.O3218 H68 2021 | DDC C813/.54—dc23

Goose Lane Editions acknowledges the generous support of the Government of Canada, the Canada Council for the Arts, and the Government of New Brunswick.

Goose Lane Editions
500 Beaverbrook Court, Suite 330
Fredericton, New Brunswick
CANADA E3B 5X4
www.gooselane.com

We are living in the time that the ancestors dreamed for us. What will we dream for the ancestors yet to come?

— Sacred Fire Foundation

No more tame language about wild things.

— Martin Shaw

HOUR OF THE CRAB

SIGNS AND PORTENTS

HOLDING PATTERNS

HOUR
OF
THE
CRAB

HOUR OF THE CRAB

Kate, walking along the beach, found the body. She was kicking pebbles into the little frothy waves and pretending. Each stone bore away a burden. *Unswept winter grit on our front steps. Stupid argument with Vikram over chair specs for that client. Missing Diane's wedding and my mother saying, You never think of—* The last pebble thunked against something sodden. There in the shallows, a few strides ahead, some tangle of something—washed in by the tide, probably. Sunlight glittered, darkening her vision. A larger wave flung the tangle closer, wrapped round a dead fish.

Not a fish.

A human foot, bloated, grey-white. Jeans plastered to thin legs. Now an arm, swollen, wound in seaweed.

She stopped on a caught breath, watching without hope for tiny movement. Only the waves moved, rocking, rocking. Hand over her mouth she bent forward. The body was slack, without tension, T-shirt holed and rotting. Narrow shoulders, flat chest—not a child but not quite an adult, either. The frilled edges of a cut on the left calf gaped.

Along the *avenida* the first of the cafés were clattering their metal fronts open. Shakily she looked up and down the beach. No one except, far off, near the rocks, holding a scoop net, an elderly fisherman who would not know English. The head lolled toward her—a face that was not a face, lips eaten away, teeth and nose coated with foam. She knelt, eyes averted, peeled the pockets apart. No ID, no cellphone, nothing. The zip of the jeans, salt-crusted, gave suddenly on a fat bleached penis. Male, she could report. If that was what she was going to do.

He must have been in the water for days. On the more intact foot was a tattoo of some sort, a stick figure—was that it?—with a triangle on either side. She puzzled over it. Smuggling? Drugs? Or nothing, just some design he'd liked. But if she went to the police... She'd heard the stories; she wasn't naive. A tiny crab scuttered from the right ear, disappeared into sand.

She'd go back to the pension instead, wake Gavin, keep her mouth shut. Let someone else find him. It wouldn't take long. Gavin, his medical residency a year behind him, now working nights in Emergency, deserved a break. She couldn't do a thing for the drowned boy, but she could protect her husband. Hadn't that been the reason for coming here—to leave the weight of duty and a just-ended Canadian winter behind?

When she reached the shop where she and Gavin had bought ice creams the evening before, something stopped and turned her. He was someone's son. Someone's brother, or lover. Somewhere people were worrying about him. Though when she walked back, the row of cars in front of the Comisaría with their sword and axe symbol made her hesitate.

—Yes, yes, we find on beach all the time, the duty officer in his rumpled shirt said, his hands splayed out. She'd finally managed to get herself inside, where he interrupted her flailing Spanish. —We pick up and make report. The body, it goes to *el depósito de cadáveres*.

All the time? They found bodies on the beach all the time?

—He is migrant. Illegal migrant. The officer was exasperated, half-contemptuous. —They come in boats, too many people, from over there—the hand flung out again—from África, from Marruecos, Túnez. Then engine breaks, they have no food, no water. Then a storm comes. He pushed angrily at a stack of papers.

Not drugs, then, but desperation or determination or reckless desire. *We pick up and make report.* His statement wasn't callous but exact. It wasn't the officer's fault the boy had come, or anyone's. In an hour or two there'd be no evidence the body had ever been there. Other people would spread out beach towels, lay their own living bodies down on the sparkling sand.

—You went for a walk? This early? Gavin was already in the bar next door to their pension, coffee and some thin biscuit on the table in front of him. Several male heads swung in Kate's direction, eyes travelling over her, talk bubbling back up as she sat down.

—I thought a walk would wake me up. She felt the prick of tears. There'd been her father's cancer, just last year, all over in seven weeks, then Gavin's brother, suicidal when they'd axed his support job at the group home. She was sick of death, desire for death. —It's beautiful, early on. So quiet.

13

No tourists at all. The barman lifted his eyebrows at her, mimed the raising of a cup.

–What do you think *we* are? Teasing, eyes softening in his sleep-creased face, hair on one side still flattened.

–Not like those — oh, *you* know. The Marthas and Henrys. Their own term for the fat ones impaled with gadgetry, the overloud voices. A pretense, really; a private snobbery.

–You look — I don't know. Subdued.

That was the trouble with marriage; once you peeled apart from each other, you were seen through. But then she'd been told all her life she had an honest face.

–What about a swim? Near that thatched bar? He meant where they'd been the day before, soon after they arrived. Not a hundred metres from where she'd found the boy.

–You go if you want. She shut her eyes and drank the last of her espresso quickly. –I'll finish unpacking. Get my things hung up.

–Come on, Kate. Out with it. Did *I* do something? He slumped back in his chair, deflated. –I thanked you, didn't I? For getting us here?

She was hanging up the new sundress in the darkened room, the shutters pulled to, when the boy surfaced. He sat up suddenly and smiled at her, his white teeth alarming. –I am sorry, I fall asleep. It was long, to swim here. He looked past her at something, perhaps the ocean; was that what he saw?

–After boat sinks. I have to try, no? His small dry laugh sounded as if he were choking. He stood, his body narrow and bony under the wet shirt, the ratty jeans. –You are from America? His face, with its fine flared nose and a dimple that came and went, was intact, smooth, beautiful.

She glanced away for a moment, breaking eye contact, reassuring herself with the solidity of shutters, night table, bed. The hanger with the sundress bit into her fingers.

–Or England, maybe. Me, I go to Germany, a brother of a friend will help. He laughed his small dry laugh again. –You come to play, *I* come to find life.

A living, was that what he meant? To make a living?

–No. A life. He jerked his head in what might have been the direction of Africa. –Over there is nothing. Nothing, walking to meet you.

She could never do what Gavin did. Saving lives was one thing, but not watching people die. As a child her sister had buried mice and sparrows in the back yard; Kate, repulsed, stayed in the house, cutting little suits out of upholstery fabric for her dolls. Now she designed furniture made from recycled materials for an energetic local business called BioHome. Her mission in life — ridiculous, really, but the idea of it sustained her — was to invent the perfect chair. Make people feel cradled, held, utterly safe. She saw her chairs stationed in every boardroom on the planet, bringing peace, happiness, goodwill.

She'd done a past-life regression once, visiting a psychic in Toronto with her old university roommate. Apparently she'd been an eighteenth-century Spanish nun, a member of the Discalced Carmelite order, no less, founded by St. Teresa of Ávila.

–A nun! Gavin said. –So that's why the saviour complex. He said it lightly, tossed off; he might be accused of the same thing, for that matter. –Let's see, your father was Jewish, your mother's lapsed Greek Orthodox—

—In the eighteenth century, Gavin. That's a long time ago. To be carrying a complex, I mean.

—Why is no one ever reincarnated from a cleaning woman? Or a—I don't know, a coal miner. Or a mugger.

Both of them had had progressive childhoods. Gavin's grandfather had been a union organizer in Winnipeg, a member of the Communist Party, and in the forties had learned Russian as preparation for moving the family to Moscow. The Stalin show trials had eventually dissuaded him, though Gavin, as a small boy, had called him Tovarish —Comrade—Gramps. Kate bore the marks of a different set of convictions. She'd been named Katharina after her Orthodox grandmother, Anna after her Jewish one—all those *a*'s!—and became Kate-Anna, then simply Kate. Her mother's mother, the Katharina, had made a pilgrimage in her seventies to the monastery whose saint's name she shared. It lay at the foot of an Egyptian mountain where, so it was said, Moses had received the Ten Commandments. Kate's grandmother had seen with her own eyes, in a hollow in the granite, the imprint of a sandalled foot.

In the afternoon, over a late Spanish lunch, she leafed through the local English-language newspaper. Properties for sale (beach-front flats, expat businesses), the arrest of a fish-and-chip shop owner for speeding, water restrictions because of the drought. Nothing about drowned migrants —oh yes. One small paragraph, near the back. A boatload of refugees, the third this week. The engine had broken down in rough seas, they'd drifted for days. Thirty-nine out of eighty-three had been rescued. The dead included seven children under four, their bodies thrown overboard by their parents. —Where are my babies? one mother kept asking the Red Cross workers.

Had *he* been on that boat? Somewhere in the continent beyond, people waited for news. Waited to hear if he'd arrived safely, if he'd met up with others, if he'd found work. When she looked up the boy was sitting there, leaning forward on his elbows, watching her as if she were deciding his fate. *Stop it,* she wanted to tell him. *Stop following me. It's your own fault. You chose to come.*

—D'you suppose they were Senegalese?

She was sitting with Gavin at the outdoor table where she'd eaten. He was looking past her at the ocean dazzle, still in his sand-caked swim trunks, she still holding the newspaper she'd read aloud from when he came back from the beach.

—They could have been from anywhere in Africa, couldn't they? Running from civil war or something.

The waiter brought a plate of fried fish and set it down in front of him.

—Sub-Saharan migrants, it says here. That man in the market back home, what's his name, Abdourahim. He says he couldn't find a wife in his village. The rich men take three or four.

She was tearing the story out, the paper soggy from her sweat-damp hands. —He offered me a necklace. Asked would I marry him. I *think* he's Senegalese.

—I've no idea, I've never talked to him. Gavin's tone was of someone speaking, with infinite patience, to a child. —Look, Kate, don't you think you're being rather morbid? It's horrible, but there's nothing we can do, is there?

Morbid. Morbidity. One of Gavin's medical terms. Death expressed as the frequency of disease in a population, as a set of statistics. Except that, set against individual lives, the statistics broke down. You couldn't measure human life that way. The boy himself would have been outraged at such abstraction, or perhaps merely indifferent.

–I wasn't going to tell you. She looked down again at the soggy newspaper. –But I found this—dead person. On the beach.

Another boy—young man—appeared later that afternoon. She was window-shopping beside a drugstore while Gavin waited to see the pharmacist; he'd forgotten to bring his inhaler. This time the ragged T-shirt, peculiarly, bore the Toronto Blue Jays logo. *Je m'appelle Joseph*, he told her. He was from Chad, from the capital, N'Djamena, where he'd had his own small tailor shop until what he called *les difficultés* broke out. The second time rebel groups destroyed his shop, he decided to flee. A cousin in Marseilles had sent him the money. He was twenty-two years old. He'd left behind a wife, Maryam, and two small children.

–*Il fallait que je vienne*, he said, spreading his hands wide—it was necessary that I come. He did not smile. He drifted past her into sunlight as Gavin came out of the drugstore, explaining—so like him!—how he and the pharmacist had fumbled through the dictionary together to find the new word: *inhalador*. He rolled the r, pleased with himself.

–They didn't say anything else? The police? Gavin had asked her earlier.

–They find them all the time. They weren't interested.

He swallowed a bit of fish and looked up at her, squinting in the blond light. –I'm sorry, Katie. Really. Sorry you had to go through all this.

But what had she gone through, really, compared to the boy? Tears pricked again; her throat flooded with heat. –They must take them somewhere. The ones who survive, I mean. Maybe someone else on the boat knew him.

–But even if. His fork paused for a moment. –I mean, what's the point?

None, except that she was being followed, hounded even, in a way she didn't understand and couldn't have explained to Gavin. –I bet they'll know at the pension. It's a small town. There must be a camp or something.

–And then what? The line of his cheek was concave with disapproval. –You want to spend the holiday at some detention centre? Anyway, it'll be heavily guarded. They won't let you in.

Where was the Gavin she knew from home? *He always listens, your husband. Really listens, not like the other doctors.* She stood up, a sleepy leg tingling into life.

–You don't have to come with me if you don't want.

–It's a vacation, Kate. You kept telling me that, over and over. Remember?

The camp, it turned out, was miles away—the woman at the pension gestured vaguely up the coast—and out of bounds, just as Gavin had said. But there was a place, the Centro de Refugiados, that helped them, though what sort of assistance they gave, the woman couldn't say. She regarded Kate with disapproval, as if Kate herself had brought the migrants. The woman who ran the Centro was Catalan, from Barcelona, did Kate know? Did she know about the Catalans and their separatist sympathies? No, of course not. Only in Spain did such nonsense occur. Only in Spain were they allowed—but the telephone rang and the woman swung away, glaring.

The Centro was a thirty-minute walk through untouristy back streets. By the time Kate rang the bell on Calle de la Gloria, the damp flannel of late-morning heat clung to her back and armpits. After a long wait, footsteps, then the grille in the door sliding open. Kate attempted an explanation.

—A moment, please, said a female voice, in overly enunciated English, and a deadbolt grated. —*Pase, pase.* I am Victoria. The top of her vigorous curls came not quite to Kate's chin; the hand with its tapered vermilion nails was as small as a child's. —We are firebombed a few months ago. That is why the lock. She laughed explosively as though it was all a joke. —I used to be journalist in Barcelona. Catalan and a *migrante* sympathizer—that is two for one, no?

In the heat Kate had become slow and baffled.

—You find body, yes, I understand, Victoria said firmly, and took Kate's arm. In the tiny office upstairs she pushed Kate into a chair, gently, as though dealing with an invalid. —I am sorry. Very—what is word?—disturbing. I know.

—There's a camp, isn't there, Kate said, and held the glass of cold water Victoria brought her to her forehead. —Where they process people. The woman at the pension told me.

—And why do you care? Victoria spoke without rancour, sitting on the edge of her desk. —It is not for sightseeing. For taking photos.

—I don't—I mean, shouldn't I care? Shouldn't everyone?

She took a deep, shuddering breath; it wasn't an answer.
–I had to. That's all.

Victoria grunted deep in her throat, like an animal. –They escape the camp, if they can. It is like a jail only worse. Then there are others, they land in secret, no one sees them. She turned and pointed through the window at the hills above them. –Up there they are hiding. Many, many. Her English seemed to be slipping further in the emotion of the moment. –In the trees, in caves. It is shaming, *vergonzoso*. Not right.

A belated honeymoon, Gavin joked; they hadn't been able to afford one four years earlier when they got married. Before coming they'd pored over the pictures of the Alhambra — the tilework, the filigree, the sunstruck fountains. The names that came from some jasmine-scented dream: the Court of the Lions, the Hall of the Two Sisters, the Gate of Pomegranates. Though the truth was it had been built by Christian slaves.

–There's an express train leaving this afternoon at two. Gavin passed her the bag of croissants he'd bought for breakfast at the bakery across the street. –And I got the name of a pension in Granada from a guy waiting to be served, he'd just been there.

He held out the guidebook, opened at those glowing photos. –The Alhambra's less crowded at night, it says here.

He was glowing himself, enthusiastic, the tiredness that lived on his face drained away. How she wanted to feel the same! Instead she said –Why don't we go tomorrow instead?

–Oh, for god's sake. The guidebook landed, with more force than necessary, on the bed between them. –It's that camp, isn't it.

–There's others, too, in hiding. I think if I went—

–It isn't just about that boy. It can't be.

–It's about— Would she know what it was about, if she went? If she met the survivors face to face? –You go, she said, if you want. It's okay with me. Really. Maybe we can go again, later on.

–There's nothing—you don't even speak the language. He flung up his hands in exasperation, like the police officer had. –Oh, hell. The hell with it. I'll go on my own.

Victoria and a man called Javier took her in the Centro's dusty van. Javier—thin, stooped, wedge of black hair above glasses—turned out to be a grad student at the University of Málaga, studying sociology and community development. He shook hands with almost religious fervour.

–We are mostly volunteer, here at the Centro, Victoria explained. –We get money, little bits, from the *parroquia*, parish I think you say, from other organizations, from people on the street even. That exploding laugh again. –Actually I am married to a migrant. She grinned at Kate's startled look. –Only, back then we say "refugees." People forget.

He was Czech, apparently; his family had escaped in '68 after the Soviets invaded. She inclined her head, ironic. –Victoria Beltrán Sokol, *a tu servicio*. Lukáš has his own law practice. Very useful. She pressed a thumb downward in the air, as if pinning some squirming official. Drove fast, one small foot flooring the accelerator, while Javier shouted history from the back seat.

–Eight years ago almost, we find, me and my brother, we find bodies, like you. At another beach, more east. He jerked his head in the direction of the dust cloud swirling behind them. –Eleven. Yes, eleven, all at once. So we form, me and Luis and Victoria, she is his girlfriend—

–Ex-girlfriend, Victoria corrected, swinging the wheel hard—a huddle of sheep billowed round the curve. She raised an eyebrow in the rearview. –Really, Javi. Such *ancient* history.

–We form support group, also pressure group, Javi said firmly, unrepentant. –We bring food, clothes, find doctors. Try to change laws. The road was twisting itself higher into the hills; Javier caught hold of the back of Kate's seat as Victoria took another curve with abandon. –Now more come, all the time, some people say is our fault. I tell to them, okay, what you want? We take them back to beach and push in water?

–At first we try to find jobs and apartments. So they can become legal. Victoria threw up a voluble, despairing hand. –All are traumatized. And no one wants them.

They were still climbing; Javier, turning, pointed to the glitter of sea far below them. –Many end up down there. That is biggest cemetery. And it has no *lápidas*—Victoria, how do you–?

–Tombstones, Victoria said.

They pulled into a sort of rough clearing, high up in the pines. As Kate got out the cooler air shocked her into alertness. Children in various stages of undress were appearing between the trees, holding plastic bowls and bottles. A clump of them stared at her in silence; others chattered round Javier, tugging at his sleeves. Victoria bent down and picked up a small girl in a dirty pink T-shirt.

–Khadija had a birthday last week, didn't you, Khadija? Victoria held up three waggling fingers. Khadija pulled her thumb from her mouth and held up three of her own, smiling uncertainly. Beyond the children dim adults moved, shadows in the deeper shadow. Plastic sheeting had been strung up here and there, bits of cardboard wedged underneath to make walls.

–Can you imagine, Victoria said. –Living in the hills like this, eating squirrels and sparrows. She shrugged, turning the gesture into a jaunty bouncing that made Khadija giggle. A kind of stupor hung over the place. Javier, children still hanging from his arms, dispensed band-aids and aspirin to a few adults, their faces guarded, expressionless. –You are here, they are more cautious, Victoria explained.

A tall greying man in too-short pants, his face an ashen black, stepped forward. –This is Nagmeldin, Victoria said as Kate held out a hand he didn't take — from fear? Embarrassment?

–He is from Sudan. He has told us different stories, how he got here. Nagmeldin said something in Spanish; Victoria clicked her tongue between her teeth. –He thinks you are some government official. I explain you are tourist.

A tourist. A Martha, even if she wasn't fat and loud. One of the lucky ones, the ones who'd won the lottery of birth and lived across the ocean and ruled the world. She put her hand behind her back, suffocated with shame. How could she tell them about a faceless dead boy, her little act of charity while on holiday? But Nagmeldin was staring at her; had Victoria said something? She looked about for a stick and knelt, drawing what she remembered of the tattoo in the loose earth. Nagmeldin squatted, murmuring, while Victoria translated.

–There were many young men on his boat. From Sudan, most of them. He says this — Victoria pointed to the drawing — is not from Sudan.

Nagmeldin rose in one uncoiling movement and began speaking emphatically, hands animated, something to do with papers, documents. He was thirty-nine, too old to have come here. Back home soldiers had killed his wife, his four children, two of his brothers. Home, in fact, no longer existed. He shut his bloodshot eyes and opened them again.

–He thinks you have come to offer jobs, Victoria said.

–We ask someone else. Javier retrieved his arm from a small boy, nostrils clogged with mucus. –Jamila, maybe— she knows everything.

An old woman in a headscarf, one arm shrivelled, squatted on the ground, stirring something over an open fire. –We bought them camping stoves but they don't use, Victoria said, lips thinned in exasperation. She pointed to blackened trees at the edge of the clearing. –Last month a shelter burns. Three of them go to hospital, then the police deport. We are lucky no one dies.

Kate bent and drew the tattoo on the ground again. Jamila nodded vigorously, jabbing her finger as her husband, small and rheumy-eyed, explained in some mix of languages. –Berber, they say, Victoria said, straightening. –From Morocco, like them. But not on a boy. Only Berber women have tattoos.

–An illiterate boy from the mountains. The woman who spoke, in startlingly fluid English, stood apart from the others, a tall figure enfolded in a miraculously clean shawl. –The er-Rif Mountains, in the north. Perhaps you know of. Glancing at Kate with contempt, face thin and alert.

–He was on your boat? Kate said, suddenly riveted.

But the woman flung a fierce look at Victoria instead. –Why does she care? What is this boy to us? She pulled the shawl tighter, outlining her swollen belly. –The sea took my husband, does she know that? Does she know my child has no father? Her bangled arm swung recklessly round the encampment. —The dead, at least, are at peace. But the living... Who cares about us?

In the silence Javier stepped forward, offering oranges and milk to the crowd around them. Khadija, given the important task of carrying food to her family, staggered off, beaming. The tall woman folded the items in her shawl with offended dignity; Jamila, still stirring her pot, spat on the ground.

—Can you tell us more? Victoria said quietly. —About this boy?

The woman shrugged, looking past them. —My husband tell me to hold onto boat, I don't know how long, many hours. A fishing boat saves me. We had nothing, no food, nothing. Too many people. The boat tips over.

—And the boy? Victoria said again, so softly Kate could barely hear her.

He had been among many others, waiting to cross. The men teased him about his woman's tattoo. Had boarded some patched-together thing riding low in the water. What had happened to him she had no idea. When Kate asked for his name she flapped her hand, as if brushing off flies. The tattoo had been his mother's idea, to protect him from *jnoun* — the evil spirits that entered the body from the ground in a strange country.

—*Azemmur*, Jamila said suddenly, insistently, pointing at the drawing again. —*Azemmur*. The husband said something to the woman with the shawl, who listened with a kind of angry indifference.

—They say it is olive tree, she said, still staring at something beyond them all. —Olive tree between two mountains, for strength. She shrugged again, dismissing them. —That is name they use in their language, but true name is *al-zeitoun*. It is Arabs who long ago bring olive tree to this country.

Ø

On the way back Javier drove; Victoria sat slumped in the back seat, hands filled with scrawled notes, photographs, even a résumé, written in what turned out to be badly spelled French. She and Javier talked desultorily in Spanish, of which Kate caught only the odd word: *una semana, claro que sí, nada más.* She turned toward the back seat when it seemed, for a moment, opportune. —Who is she, that woman? Why's she here?

Victoria opened her laptop and began tapping something into it. —She is from wealthy family in Fez. Educated, her father is professor. Victoria squinted at one of the strewn notes, then tapped some more. —Zainab, her name is. She is supposed to marry but she fall in love with cousin. Poor cousin. They run away. Now she want to go back, but she know her family will not accept.

There she had stood, wrapped in her shawl, holding her milk and oranges above her belly, her face angry and astonished as though she hadn't expected the world to fail her so dramatically.

—Tomorrow, Javier said, we organize a big dinner. We take food and cook with them. You want to come?

She couldn't risk another argument with Gavin. Besides, they were going to a fiesta in a village whose name she couldn't remember, farther along the coast, where locals in authentic costumes re-enacted the Christian conquest of the Moors.

—How many people survived from Zainab's boat?

—Who knows? A muscle in Javier's jaw flickered. —Maybe the police catch others.

Victoria, behind them, gave another of her animal grunts. —Police hold for sixty days, if they find, and then they deport. The grunt changed to a snorting laugh. —And then there is Zainab. She *want* to go back but she cannot. Ironic, no?

Two a.m. and she couldn't sleep, though Gavin was snoring lightly through his open mouth. This time the boy's name was Drissa and he came from Mali. He was seventeen years old, with high cheekbones and an insouciant smile. He wore a faded green shirt that was far too big for him and rope-soled sandals. He'd spent twelve days in a boat trying to reach Spain; he was hoping to get a job in the vast plastic greenhouses along the coast. His father was dead, his mother ill, he needed money to support five siblings. With that smile of his, Europe, beckoning and golden, would open its arms and embrace him.

The bus, when she boarded it that morning — a newer one, apparently, was out of service — had sprung seats and a defeated air. Across the aisle an elderly woman in black pulled her headscarf over her face Arab-style as Kate sat down. She'd left Gavin a note telling him where she was going. Envied him his ability — honed at his job? — to fall immediately into oblivion, to sleep as if he deserved it. Well, he did, didn't he?

Despite two *cafés solos* she felt foggy and dislocated. A crucifix swung wildly from the rearview on each hairpin curve, providing apparent protection, though she already knew she'd arrive safely. Azemmur, as he now was, was depending on her. From the Málaga bus station a taxi bore her through the gold varnish of late morning, needling in and out of heavy traffic. The red Moroccan flag with its five-pointed star hung from a nondescript building in a street filled with consulates—Germany, Ecuador, Ukraine.

—We arrest those who profit from such trafficking, the consul told her, a tall and dignified man in his precise European suit. He was evidently under the impression she'd travelled all the way from Canada to correct this wrong, a misapprehension she couldn't seem to alter. —Also we have campaigns on TV, warnings. His finely lashed eyes closed and opened again. —But they think we are lying, the migrants. They believe those who came earlier, who maybe were given amnesty.

He had decided she was there not to find a name but to lodge a complaint. Tourists, especially North American ones, needed to be appeased, to be comforted like children. She laid before him the tattoo she'd drawn on a piece of paper.

—Yes, yes, it could be an olive tree. It could be anything. He shrugged. —I grew up in Casablanca, I went to L'Institut d'Études Politiques in Paris. These—he pushed the paper back to her—are village beliefs, you understand. I have no knowledge of such things.

They occupied the same world, she and the consul. They lived in one world and the boy and Zainab and Nagmeldin in another, and there was no bridge between them. Gavin, sensible Gavin, must be driving, elbow resting on the open window, along the turquoise coast, past those miles of green-houses under plastic, to that village where they pretended to murder each other with swords and scimitars. She was almost out the door when the consul called after her.

—Go to the port. There are Moroccans working there. Someone might be able to help.

Ø

A bulky man in a hardhat and safety vest came toward her, eyes performing a practised flick down and up her body. Two o'clock, oppressively hot, men and equipment unloading a container ship tall as a skyscraper, the *BF Leticia*. The smell of oil, rubber, hot tar.

—I'm looking for someone, she shouted over the clangs and rumbles. —Someone who might know a boy from the Rif Mountains.

The foreman, if that was who he was, grinned, white teeth impertinent. —In those mountains are many villages. If you don't know village... He struck the drawing lightly with his fingers, contemptuous, suspecting something, something sexual; his nostrils flared, avid. —How you know this boy?

—I found his body. On the beach. He came in one of those boats.

The nostrils contracted; the man stared, taken aback. —I call Marouane. Okay? He is from er-Rif.

Marouane could not have been more than fifteen, wiry and underfed; an eyelid flickered nervously. The foreman translated. Men went looking for work, Marouane said, from all the mountain villages—from Azilane and Akchour and Abou Bnar. Brothers, cousins, uncles, now scattered through Germany, Spain, France. In some of the villages only women and children were left. He knew nothing about some Rifi man with a tattoo. If he had died, then Allah had willed it. He stared at her, astonished that an American could travel so far and know so little.

Gavin was in the bar next door, his head turned, like the other men's, to the TV and the soccer game. The fiesta had been wonderful, he said without moving; she should have come. People dressed in jewelled turbans, in silver armour incised with crescents, or wearing white tabards with red crosses, carrying dragon-emblazoned shields. The captain of the Moors rode a real camel through the streets. A commercial came on; Gavin, turning, was exuberant, still caught up in the game. –Stupid, that argument, he said. He was being contrite, generous—the Gavin she knew again. –We can go back if you want. The village. It's a pretty place.

He didn't ask about her trip. Perhaps he didn't want to know. The tight band across her chest loosened a little.

–Would you mind? she said. –Another day on your own? I have something else to do tomorrow.

He stared at her, eyes narrowing. –You sure you know what you're getting into?

She glanced at the resumed game, pretending interest. –I'll need the car, she said, not meeting his eyes. –And don't ask more questions! Playful, a little flirtatious, the way they were when one of them wanted, unaccompanied, to buy a gift for the other. She put a hand out, to soften the abruptness. –You stay here, go to the beach. It doesn't need two of us. Besides, they already know me.

–You mean at the camp? he said. –Don't do anything stupid.

Victoria was on her phone, sitting on her desk among files and papers, glasses pushed up into her curls. –What did you expect? she said when Kate had finished her story, and then, more kindly: —I know, you want to try. So did we, at the beginning.

Es una tonta, she would probably tell Javier later. A spoiled kid, *una caprichosa*.

—Look, you want a coffee? I have some news.

Zainab, it turned out, had remembered the name of the boy's village, or so she claimed. She'd told Javier so at the dinner the evening before. In the bar across the street Victoria ordered two *cafés solos* and sat down. —She will tell only if we take her to ferry to Morocco.

—She's blackmailing us, then.

Victoria tore open a paper tube of sugar, shrugging. —She want to deliver baby there.

—But why?

In Zainab's position the last place Kate would have gone was back to Morocco.

—She say is only bad luck here.

—Then why doesn't she go to the police and get deported?

—She thinks they beat her. Or kill her. Last month they are putting man on plane to Tunisia, he dies. Victoria shrugged again, as if such run-of-the-mill tragedy was the way of the world now. Which it probably was.

—The baby'll have Spanish citizenship if she stays, won't it?

A myth, unfortunately, or so Victoria said, though pregnant women arrived every day believing it was true. —Baby will be Moroccan. But Lukáš will help, and others. She is a widow, educated... Victoria stared out the window, as if already marshalling arguments against an adamantine bureaucracy. —She perhaps have chance. If she tell good story.

—*You're* not going to take her, are you?

—*¡Claro que no!* Victoria looked horrified. —It is dangerous. For us, of course, but also for her. If she is caught...
She gave Kate a sharp, narrowed stare. —She think we can
get whatever we want. Especially you. You would do same
thing, no, in her position?

—So she thinks *I'll* help her do this? Kate stared back,
thrilled at Zainab's audacity, at what she had seen, or intuited,
in Kate.

—She has friend in Casablanca, woman, American woman.
Victoria pushed away the half-drunk coffee, frowning. —She
say she will go there.

—But if she doesn't have a passport...

—She will find truck, Moroccan truck, going on ferry. Ask
driver to hide her. Victoria threw a handful of coins on the
table, over Kate's protestations. —You can pay when we learn
name of village. If we learn. Javi goes tomorrow with doctor
who works with us, Zainab likes her. Javi will ask again.

Finding the clearing on her own wasn't easy, though she
remembered the turnoff, some ten kilometres or so beyond
the town, the road that wound steeply upward and narrowed
into packed earth. Though it lengthened beyond all reason
and she almost turned back. She passed no one except a
boy on a mountain bike, flying down. After several wrong
guesses, the clearing at last revealed itself and she pulled
over, breathless with risk in the rental car that advertised
her as a visitor.

The children came running before she'd turned off the
ignition. She passed out several chocolate bars from the stash
in the glove compartment to small grabbing hands. Two or

three older boys stood at a wary distance, smoking. From the trunk she hauled out her backpack and the box of groceries she'd bought just before leaving town. Those who'd lost out on the chocolate clamoured round her, shoving and pushing.

–Can you help, please? she called to the distant boys, but no one moved. Fortunately here was Nagmeldin, coming down the path with a limp Kate hadn't noticed before.

–I thought you could use — you know. Could hand this out to everyone. She gestured weakly at the box, which Nagmeldin stooped for and swung to his shoulder. The children, ebullient, danced round, the boys throwing mock punches at each other. They'd only gone a few steps when Nagmeldin made a chopping motion toward her, hand held sideways.

–Okay. You go now.

She stopped, stupid with surprise. He hadn't even said thank you. She was a friend, wasn't she? — a friend of friends? Or did he think it was dangerous, her presence — though it was a risk when the Centro people came too. The children drifted after him, glancing back with cool indifference.

She wasn't leaving, of course — she had a delivery to make. In her daypack were little jars of preserved lemon, Moroccan spices with exotic names — *karfa*, *skinjbir*, *tahmira* — that she'd pounced on in the supermarket. An exchange of sorts, though she wouldn't put it like that to Zainab. Nagmeldin might be annoyed, angry even, but he couldn't stop her.

She'd gone only a few steps farther when Zainab herself burst out of the trees, panting, clutching a plastic bag to her chest. –You came! You came! She pushed past an astonished Kate and broke into an awkward run. The children surged behind them. Zainab, reaching the car, threw herself in and locked the door.

—I can't take you, Zainab, I can't! Kate shouted, arriving seconds too late and seizing the handle.

But Zainab would not get out even when Kate got the door open. The children laughed and gibbered and danced about, enchanted with the absurdity of it all. Kate implored, threatened, grabbed Zainab's arm and pulled. Zainab herself sat in a bubble of calm, looking straight ahead.

—All right. I'll take you as far as the town. Understand?

No response. Kate swore softly under her breath. She started the car and swung round onto the road in the direction of town. The children raced after them, dropping back into the boil of dust as the car gained speed.

—You came, Zainab repeated simply. —Since I arrive I pray, all day, every day. And now, *insh'allah*, I will get home.

—You understand, don't you? Kate said when they reached the junction with the main road. —That I'm dropping you in town?

Ahead of them was the highway, glinting with those trick pools of water in the afternoon sun. It wasn't her problem, it was Zainab's. She'd take her to the Centro and ask them to reason with her. Get her out of the car, at least.

Then she remembered it was Friday. The Centro closed at one p.m.

—Where were you? Gavin said irritably. He was lying on the bed, reading a paperback. Held out his watch, as if she could read it from that distance. —It's almost four.

—I know, I'm sorry, I thought I'd be back earlier. Though she hadn't in fact said so. She kicked a sandal off viciously. —There's a woman in the car.

He rose on an elbow, staring.

—She's from that camp. She wants to go back to Morocco. The hell with it, trying to be careful.

—She got in the car and I couldn't get her out. Her voice rose. —Don't ask *questions*, Gavin.

He'd swung his feet to the floor and stood up. She stood up straighter; that way they were even. —She got in the car, he said carefully, slowly. —And what? We're supposed to take her somewhere?

—She won't get out. She's pregnant, Kate added, as if that was a factor in her inability to remove Zainab, which perhaps it was. —I parked two blocks away. She doesn't know where we're staying.

—Suppose she's gone to the police to report you? He stood with his arms folded, judgemental. —Or that Centro? If you're going behind their backs.

It hadn't occurred to her that Zainab might believe she had information she could use.

—She's afraid of them. How dare he criticize her good deed? —Besides, I took some food up there, to the camp.

—In our rental car. With easily traceable plates.

Maybe he was jealous. At least she'd *tried*. Taken a risk an earlier Gavin would have applauded, back when he'd talked about working for Doctors Without Borders after medical school. —Why do you care, anyway? she said wildly, incontinently. —You didn't before.

Gavin flung the paperback on the bed—he seemed to be making a habit of flinging things—and grabbed his daypack.

—We'd better go find her, he said. —Make sure she's okay.

She was where Kate had left her, sitting in the shaded passenger seat, staring straight ahead. Gavin, bending down at the partly opened window, made her startle. He said something that Kate, a short distance away, feeling small and helpless, couldn't hear. But she heard Zainab's reply.

–You take me to ferry, please. For the first time Zainab's voice trembled, then solidified. –Only to ferry, nothing more. Please. I am begging.

She was staring up at Gavin, crumpling a corner of shawl in her hands. They'd trapped him into something, his wife and Zainab — that must be what he was thinking. He gave an almost imperceptible shrug. Walked round to the driver's side, body rigid, face held away.

They drove with the windows rolled down, Kate breathing sea air deeply, in and out. Zainab sat with her fingers splayed on her belly, her posture steely. –I am thinking, she announced out of nowhere, about names. For baby.

What did she think this was, a Sunday drive? –We're taking a big risk, you know, Kate said, her voice shaking. Gavin shot her a warning glance in the rearview.

–Karim if it is boy, Zainab said, as though Kate hadn't spoken. –It means giving, generous. And Abdellatif after my husband. Abdellatif — I don't know in English. Means something like servant of Allah.

–We'll drop you, Gavin said (he was carrying on the other conversation, the one they ought to be having), on the outskirts of town. That's safer for all of us. You can make your own way from there.

But Zainab wanted to disappear into crowds somewhere, somewhere no one would notice. The back of Gavin's neck reddened, though this time Kate agreed with her. The sun bore down on them, a dagger, striking sparks.

—I am very angry, at first, Zainab said firmly. Angry at her desperate situation? Her husband's death? —With Allah, I mean. After what happened to me, to us. Then, you know, I accept. I accept because my husband would say to do.

Kate glanced at her, appalled. She was still obeying her husband — she, an educated widow? Zainab laughed unexpectedly and threw up her hands.

—I find myself on very strange journey. Not here, to Spain — I mean *here*. She pressed a hand to her heart. —I meet my husband at wedding, big family wedding. My family already has picked out someone, very nice, engineer, good-looking.

She lifted her palms up, as if she found her own behaviour inexplicable. —But then I meet Abdellatif, he is son of my mother's cousin. My family is horrified. He is too young for me, only twenty-two, he is not educated like me at university, he is carpenter, son of a *shaikh*. A teacher of Islam, a Sufi. My father is professor at University of Al-Karaouine, he does not practise religion.

Zainab let her hands crumple on her thighs, saddened perhaps by her own conduct, or her father's. —I cannot help. I am in love. So we run away, we are married secretly. We are together only a year but I learn a lot from him.

A year. So little time. What did Allah think he was doing, leaving Zainab to fend for herself? —Who knows why? Zainab said, as if answering Kate's question. —But at least I have baby. I hope is boy like his father. But I am happy for girl, too.

—Then why don't you stay here? Gavin said, in his blunt way. —What are you going back for? The road was climbing again, the shot silk of the Mediterranean spread out below them.

—I *hate* here. That air of hostility, flooding the car. —We live, back there, like animals. Lower than animals. Only Victoria and Javier help.

—And me, Kate said quietly.

—Yes, and you. You and your husband. You are my—she pressed her hand to her heart again—my *mala'ikah*. My angels.

Gavin would be rolling his eyes, so she rushed into her question. —Before you go you must tell me the name of that village.

Zainab, puzzled, spread her hands. —I do not—

—The boy. That boy from the Rif Mountains—you said—

—Ah yes. She smiled at Kate, turning round to touch her knee. —I think was Bouazzoun. Near Taounate. Or was it Bourdoud? She paused, frowning. —My great-grandfather came from there, long ago. Yes, Bourdoud, I am sure of it now. Tiny place just past Aïn Aïcha.

They dropped her on a crowded street in the city centre, car horns shrilling behind them. Zainab walked away without looking back, just another Arab woman in a djellaba and headscarf. Why hadn't Kate asked Zainab the name of the place they'd left from, she and the boy? Unless, of course, she'd simply made it up. Not the village, but the fact of the encounter.

—We can't just abandon her, Gavin said, watching her go. —Suppose the police stop her? Or, I don't know, someone harasses her.

Over Kate's objections they followed at a distance until they lost her, turning down an alleyway. In a café, picking at a sandwich, Gavin was silent, so Kate typed the names

Zainab had given her into her phone. Nothing, though she tried several spellings. Too small, probably. Tiny sunbaked places where old men sat smoking kif.

—We can't go back, Gavin said.

—You mean the hotel?

—I mean home. Not until we look for that boy's family.

He let out a long slow breath and stood up.

—We're in it now, aren't we? We brought her here. She decided for us.

They managed to get an evening ferry after a passenger with a reservation failed to show. Gavin went off to wander the decks, or perhaps keep an eye out for Zainab, while Kate stayed in the car. In the next lane a boy in his teens was staring down at her from the cab of a truck lettered in Arabic. Thin brown face, dark-rimmed eyes—Azemmur himself. He grinned and flickered his tongue, wetting his lips. Made a circle of thumb and forefinger and jabbed the other forefinger through, back and forth.

Not Azemmur after all. Or Azemmur as he might have been, flagrant, strutting. She saw the lips parted on sharp white teeth as she turned away.

—You need advice, perhaps? Help?

Some blond foreigner in sunglasses and Moroccan shirt had stopped beside them under the awning of the café. They were drinking *qahwa helib,* café au lait, and trying to wake up; the cries of the muezzins had woken them at three a.m. The man gestured at the map Kate had spread out on the table. Did he know where Bourdoud was, she asked, near Aïn Aïcha? They were looking for someone. She brought out the sketch of the tattoo.

—You must not go to the Rif, the man said. He was German, or at least German-born; his name was Henk. He had lived in Morocco for thirty years. —The police will arrest you. They will think you are there to buy marijuana. Your story about the boy—he frowned, drawing down his mouth—they will not believe you. Men in the Rif do not wear tattoos.

Meanwhile, would they like to join him for breakfast? For the best *khobz belbid*—French toast, made with orange juice—in the city?

The restaurant, a ten-minute walk away, faced a square with a blue-tiled fountain where men stood or sat in groups, smoking, gesticulating, drinking mint tea. —Here, Henk said softly as they ate, is where you come if you want to leave. Where the fixers find you a way out. He nodded in the direction of Europe. —But it's expensive. Two thousand American dollars at least. Fifteen thousand dirhams. Your boy's family would have pooled their savings, asked relatives. Sold more kif.

Most of the men wouldn't talk, but a younger one about Kate's age, eager to practise English, told them the boy would have met the boat on some empty patch of beach farther down the coast. Near Fnideq, maybe, or Oued Laou, and probably at night. —Too many coast guard here, he explained. He himself had tried crossing, twice, and been sent back. He was from a poor village; there were no jobs there. Yes, he would try again when he'd saved the money. He eked out a living doing odd jobs. He looked out at the Strait of Gibraltar, at what Henk called the *Bab al-Maghreb*, the Gate of the Maghreb.

—Everyone knows the risks, the younger man said. —But to die once is better than dying ten times in the face of your parents' pity.

∅

Oued Laou was only sixty kilometres away, but a drive of at least two hours because of road construction. They set out in the car, the three of them, in the stinking heat, Henk having offered to come along as translator and guide. Suicidal motorbikes, their riders' shirts flapping behind them, zipped in and out. A donkey plodded past in the dust, laden with electric fans. Across the Alborán Sea, Spain shimmered dizzily.

Henk was vague about what he did. People hired him to make maquettes for building projects, designs, that sort of thing—enough to live well in Moroccan terms. He was fifty-six. In Germany there was nothing left for him. What kept him here? The intensity, the way people lived every moment as if it was their last. He pointed out the window, naming trees, birds, even dust-covered weeds. Germany lived, still, under the shadow of the war his father had fought in, on the wrong side.

On the edge of town, almost four hours later, they were directed to a wooden doorway and a man in a shabby brown suit, slender and wary, who sat drinking coffee. Yes, he could get someone to Spain, for the right price, though he brushed away the tattoo. *Mille des personnes*, he said wearily, translating into Spanish for good measure. He couldn't possibly remember them all. Yes, some of them died, but that was their fate, or the fault of the boat owners. He was simply supplying a service. No, he didn't want to go himself. The Spaniards had thrown them out, centuries ago, though the Arabs had given them everything—mathematics, running water, the names of stars. There was gratitude for you!

Gavin, over lamb tagine and wine, argued for going back.

–We're not getting anywhere. If we leave now we might just make an evening ferry.

–But we've only just started. Haven't we, Henk? We're not even in the Rif yet.

–Excuse us, Gavin said, rudely, before Henk could answer, and walked Kate outside.

–Kate. Katie. He took her hands in his. –I know you want to help, and it's wonderful of you. I know I said we should come. But it's pointless, what we're doing, don't you see?

So it had all been a ruse, their coming. She would see how silly it was and then they'd go back to their holiday. Pretend she'd never seen a dead boy on the beach.

–He chose me to find his family, she said simply. –Your science doesn't explain everything, does it. He's relying on me.

After dinner they found a budget hotel with an empty room on the third floor where they could thrash things out. Henk knew the owner — he seemed to know everyone — and said he'd sleep on the roof. He was at Kate's service if she wanted to go on, he said.

–I'm free at the moment, he told them. –No ulterior motives, it goes without saying. He flung up his hands as if they'd pointed a gun at him. –But you can't go on your own, Kate.

She and Gavin argued for most of the night as the moon bore down, an interrogation light. She'd be safe with Henk, she said, he knew the ropes. Gavin, explosive, said it wasn't about Henk, it had nothing to do with Henk. –Promise me, Katie, you'll be back by the time we fly home. Five days.

—I can't, Gav. But I'll let you know one way or the other.

Gavin put his head in his hands. —This is crazy. You do know that, don't you?

—It's not my choice. I told you already. She leaned forward and kissed the top of his head, the hair damp with sweat. —Take the car, she said. —Leave early. Maybe you'll make the ferry before the roadwork starts.

She and Henk waited two hours for the bus that would take them into the mountains. There were no spare seats. They stood pressed among men with roped bundles, the odd djellaba'd woman, half a dozen live chickens. Much later, among a handful of houses that might have been a village, Henk indicated they should get off. —You must look as though you belong to a man, he said, and took her arm as if they were a couple. She hung on gratefully, limp with the standing, the heat, the smell of dust and sweat.

Her drawing was passed from hand to hand among the old men who gathered, frowning under their headwraps. —They're telling us what we already know, Henk explained. —That it's a tattoo, what it means. Though they say it's not accurate.

A younger man appeared with a ballpoint, an older man made careful corrections, pausing, pursing his lips. Women brought plates of *kefta* and couscous, eyeing Kate with open disapproval.

The next village required a battered taxi that flung itself up a mountain round hairpin curves, each moment on the cliff edge an eternity. On the single street an ancient woman, evidently deaf, stared at them in astonishment from a doorway while several children peered round her. No one else seemed to be about. Henk took off his hat and wiped his forehead with his sleeve. To Kate's relief a boy appeared, leading a donkey. Everyone was away at some religious festival, he told Henk, who arranged to hire the donkey to carry them, or rather her, along an uphill goat track to the next village.

They arrived as the sun was setting. Another handful of buildings that seemed to have assembled themselves out of the arid pastures — she'd never seen life so stripped to its basics. The place glowed with evening light; a bat flapped past her head. They were offered a couple of mattresses in one of the houses, where a middle-aged woman with the grave face of a saint brought them some sort of bean soup and bread to scoop it up with. Afterwards Kate took a blanket and lay outside as the stars, in their brilliant indifference, came out, one by one.

In the fifth — or was it the sixth? — village, a young woman appeared who knew some English. She seemed to emerge from a group of chattering children and offered Kate a glass of what turned out to be fresh lemonade. Together with an older woman she guided Kate into the dimness of a shuttered room with a low bed, where she must have fallen asleep because the sun was setting when she woke. She made her way, groggily, toward the voices outside.

Henk was sitting at a wooden table beneath a scrawny tree, talking to an ancient man who sat leaning on a cane. The young woman she'd seen earlier was setting out cups and a pot of coffee before them, turning to Kate with the tray in her hand. Had Kate slept, was she hungry? The woman went inside and came back with a filled plate, pointing to a bench

by the house wall where Kate might sit. So she was to eat sep-
arately from the men. Or perhaps the woman wanted to talk.

Her name was Lalla; she was the daughter of the house,
visiting from the city. Her tight jeans, her long red nails
belonged elsewhere, that was clear, despite the headscarf.
–So you found a body, she said, arms folded, leaning against
the doorway of the house as Kate sat eating. –You came all
this way because you found a body?

Kate, mouth full of couscous, nodded, though with the
food warming her belly she'd half-forgotten Azemmur. Lalla
produced a cigarette, lit it, blew out smoke. Her own brother
had gone missing in Spain seven years before. He was the
oldest, expected to provide for his parents and younger
siblings. Her father believed he'd taken up with a foreign girl
and was keeping all his money for himself. Had denounced
him, publicly, stating that his son was no longer his son, that
in fact he'd never existed.

–So I went to Fez to look for work, after we didn't hear
from him. I was lucky, I knew some English, I got a job in
a hotel.

Now it was one of her younger brothers who wanted
out. He'd go to Spain next year most likely, when he turned
sixteen, or the year after that. He came up to them as Lalla
spoke, a startlingly handsome boy with thick eyelashes and
a shy smile. Said something to his sister, who frowned and
flicked her fingers at him and turned away.

–It is time for our English lesson, she told Kate. –He is
always saying English, English. Perhaps I am helping him
drown, too. But what choice did her family have? –Even the
goats here have nothing to eat, with the drought, she said.

She swept her arm across the hillside and gave Kate a
look of undisguised envy. –You know any man in Morocco

would marry you in an instant, don't you? Just like that—
she snapped her fingers. —And here *you* are, looking for a
man who doesn't even belong to you.

In the morning Lalla took her from house to house. In
each Kate held out the drawing, smudged and torn from
handling. In each the answer was the same. No, they
knew of no such boy. It was doubtful, indeed, that such a
boy existed, one whose mother would have him tattooed
like that. What boy would agree to such a thing? What
father? Not for the first time Kate wondered about Zainab's
explanation, the one she said the boy himself had given.
Perhaps, like the boy's home village, that too was made up.

Instead they told her about their own sons, the ones
they'd lost to that narrow strait that separated Morocco from
the continent. They held out photographs, they cried names
aloud, they called on Allah as witness. In the last house an
aging woman who must once have been a beauty took a
framed photograph surrounded by candles from an alcove,
kissed it, then held it out to Kate. A child still, the boy in the
photograph, with his downy face and dreamy eyes. He'd left
when he was seventeen, the woman said as Lalla translated.
—He's thirty-seven now, if he's still alive, *insh'allah*. Here,
take, you take. And she thrust the photo into Kate's hands,
refusing to take it back. —Look for this boy instead. He's
still alive, I'm sure of it. I have a little money, I can pay. And
she fumbled coins from her kaftan, though Kate held her
other hand behind her back. It was Lalla who intervened,
who handed the photo back to the woman and said to Kate
—Don't you dare take him on. Go home. Find your husband.

In the morning Kate couldn't even keep water down. A pair of implacable hands had taken hold of her gut, twisting, twisting. She writhed under the sheet, wanting Gavin, wanting the safety of her own room in distant Canada. Lalla's mother came in and bathed her forehead and hands with rosewater. Henk came in too—she heard his voice from a long way away, speaking to the mother in Arabic. A surge of deep longing for something rolled over her. She vomited into a basin.

Later she dozed from time to time, jerked out of sleep by noises, by dreams. Once she was better she would search until Azemmur told her to stop. She'd met his family, or people who might as well have been his family, in all these little villages—cousins and grandparents, sisters and aunts. She'd eaten their food, slept on their straw mattresses. They'd asked their god to bless her journey, they urged her to let them know if she found the boy's family. Like all the others he had left for an unknown country, one with no passports, no immigration controls. An underwater country populated by the dead. They lay among the waving seaweed, the fat darting fish.

Toward evening Azemmur came. He was bathed in a kind of shining radiance. He lit a candle that seemed to be floating on a bowl of fragrant oil. –I am grateful, *khti*, he told her gently, but you will not find me. He turned, then, and walked toward an ocean she hadn't noticed until now. She wept and pleaded but he moved resolutely on. She sat down on the sand, cold and shaking, and watched him until his head disappeared beneath the waves.

She woke to voices—Henk and someone else—discussing something in hushed tones. Someone, a woman she had never seen before, came in and held a concoction of bitter herbs to her lips. Perhaps she was dying, though she didn't think so. She had been granted a glimpse across a border, that was all. Gavin had seen the Alhambra and the village where the Moors fought the Christians, but the place she had seen was in no guidebook that she knew of. Azemmur had led the way, and she had followed. A thin line of radiance lingered just below the shutters, where the ocean had seeped in.

HAPPINESS

As always he strapped on his duty belt with its baton and flashlight, slid the pistol into its holster, adjusted the *gorra* to its exact position in the mirror. Luisa teased him sometimes, said he was vain as any woman, but precision was what he'd learned thirty-four years ago as a young recruit and he couldn't change now. In the hallway he kissed her cheek, as he always did, and as always she patted his arm and invoked unearthly protection. *—Que Dios te traiga a casa seguramente.* He was grateful for the benediction, though he wasn't a believer; maybe it had kept him safe all these years. Marisol, texting on her phone, didn't even look up when he opened the front door.

Already his radio was crackling as he slid into the driver's seat. Another boatload of migrants, twenty kilometres off the coast near Marbella. That meant another interception, the third this week. He hoped, this time, there were no corpses. Twenty years ago, when he'd transferred from Highway Patrol to the glamorous new Servicio Marítimo, the posting had been his for the asking. –Why does the sea need guarding, Papá? Emilia, then six, had wanted to know. That was two months after he'd found that Algerian child, not much older than Emilia, frozen to death one brutal winter night in the undercarriage of a freight truck on the old A4 motorway just outside Seville. Three others, barely teenagers, had been crammed in as well, so inert with cold they couldn't walk.

At the station he watched the progress of the migrant boat on the closed-circuit TV, then turned to his paperwork. In thirty-four years he'd never caught up. At night sometimes he sat knee-deep in paper at a desk, trying to beat off more sheets snowing down from the sky. He'd resisted the promotion to captain until his superintendent had phoned from headquarters and told him he was getting his third star whether he liked it or not. –There's a fourth star, too, *capitán* Hortelano, his sergeant, Arregui, told him, grinning. –For meritorious execution of paperwork over a lifetime. Measured in reams.

Marisol, twelve then, had said it was cool and called him *papá de las estrellas*. Felipe, who'd already made it clear he wasn't following his father into the force, even tried on the jacket with its brand-new epaulets.

Just after nine he downed a *café solo* in the bar next door and headed to the dock with Arregui. The rescue boat was reporting fifty-seven migrants, including nine women and seven kids. They were nearly always in rough shape, the *ilegales*—dehydrated, starving, sunburnt. At dockside they were joined by three nurses from the Red Cross. Arregui's radio crackled again and Hortelano listened in. There was a tenth woman, lying at the back of the boat on sodden blankets. She'd just given birth.

Arregui whistled through his teeth. —What does that make the baby, *jefe*? A citizen of the Mediterranean?

—Work for lawyers. Hortelano stood watching as the rescue boat entered the harbour, black-skinned figures draped in blankets at the railings, the usual battered dinghy in tow. Fishers of men, Christ had said, though in his own case it wasn't for souls but for bodies, on behalf of the Spanish government. Why had that phrase from his long-ago catechism classes suddenly surfaced?

Cabo Pilar Meléndez Cardozo, the new badge of a lance corporal on her shirt sleeve, was pulling on her latex gloves and talking to the nurses. He still found it awkward, calling her by her last name — women weren't allowed to join the force in his day — but he was glad she was here. Pilar had a calming effect on the migrants. On her first interception she'd wept, afterwards, in his office, blowing her nose angrily in a tissue. —I'm sorry, I'm sorry.

—Don't, he told her. —Don't apologize. But don't take it home with you, either.

She was twenty-six, the same age, incredibly, as Emilia was now, and he'd wanted to put his arm round her and tell her everything would be all right.

The boat was nosing into dock, a dozen or more other SEMAR members standing by, plus immigration officers and military police. Pilar and Arregui climbed on board to talk to the crew who'd carried out the apprehension. How many migrants had he interviewed over the years — thousands? Tens of thousands? They were helped ashore, one by one, most of them younger males in hoodies or woollen caps, the few women in robes or jeans. The woman who'd just given birth was carried off by stretcher, followed by Pilar holding a bundle that suddenly waved a fist and gave a sharp catlike cry.

–Look, *jefe*, look! She came hurrying over to show him.

–She's fine, she's healthy, at first I thought she'd—Breaking off, biting her lip as Hortelano reached out and lifted the baby from her. Body memory took over, making a cradle of his arms. The black eyes were bright but the skin was cool, the umbilical cord still dangling from the cloths that held her. Without thinking he unfastened his vest to zip her inside, the tiny heart fluttering birdlike against his own.

Arregui phoned him that evening, as he'd asked. The baby's parents were from Nigeria. The mother was nineteen. They'd walked to Morocco—it had taken them six months—where they'd paid a *tiburón*, a shark, to arrange passage across the *mar de Alborán*, the western Mediterranean. The baby had been born half an hour before the rescue boat found them.

In the morning, after he left the house, he found himself driving to the hospital. The mother was anemic and badly dehydrated, so the nurse on duty told him; the baby had a severe case of oral thrush. He stared at the incubator with its tiny occupant through the viewing window, at its tubes and dials and portholes. Down the hall the mother was propped against pillows, her face taut with exhaustion. He rocked his arms, miming a cradle, folded his hands against his cheek as she watched, expressionless. –Okay, he said, slowly, loudly, leaning forward to touch her arm. –All okay.

But it wasn't. She'd probably recover, she and the baby, but she'd still be deported in sixty days. Unless she found a lawyer, and even then... It was an impossible situation. You couldn't let them all in.

–They're taking our jobs, Papá, aren't they? Marisol said that evening at dinner, in a rare burst of conversation. –Paco's dad just got laid off from his construction job. Again.

Luisa was passing round the dish of spiced potatoes. –What's got into you, Kiko, visiting babies in hospitals? She laughed, not unkindly. –She'll need clothes. I'll dig out that old layette of Marisol's.

–Papá's getting soft, said Felipe. He pushed away his plate and got up. –All right if I take the car?

"The car" meant Luisa's little Renault, the one he'd bought her last year for her fiftieth birthday. Luisa sighed theatrically. –You'll be home by midnight? Not like last night?

–Promise. Felipe kissed her cheek, already shrugging on his jacket. Slam of the door, the thud of running steps, then the car farting into life outside. Was it really thirty-odd years since he and Luisa had groped each other in some Sevillan back street in his father's elderly Volvo? He'd had a talk with Felipe when the boy turned sixteen, had even bought him some condoms. Felipe had looked at him pityingly. –This brand's useless, Papá. It always comes off.

When he went back in the morning the duty nurse, a different one, wouldn't let him in. –She was terrified after you came, she tried to leave. She isn't well.

Years ago he would have asserted his rights as an officer of the Guardia Civil, those black-tricorned police who had once terrorized rural villages but were now, in post-dictatorship Spain, redeeming themselves. Instead he returned after work, in civilian clothes. Two guards from Immigration stood outside the door of the ward, edgy. One, a young recruit named Ignacio, he knew from the docks.

–She's under guard now? Hortelano took out the package of mints that ten years ago had replaced cigarettes.

–We brought her husband in. Ignacio jerked his head toward the room. –The *jefe* said he could have an hour.

That was unusual, letting people out of detention for a hospital visit. The baby was making everyone soft. The father sat at the bedside, tall and bony in a shrunken track suit, hands dangling between his legs. The mother held the baby, who was sucking steadily at a breast. A glimpse of pinky-black nipple as she saw him and clutched, alarmed, at the blanket, the father rising warily. Hortelano patted the air in a gesture of reassurance. –Enrique, he said, pointing at himself, and slowed down the syllables. –En-ree-kay.

The father wetted his lips and mumbled something that sounded like Adbo. No, not Adbo—a vigorous head shake—Adebayo. He gestured at his wife. –Olabisi. And this one—he spoke in English, laying his large hand on the baby's head—this one bring us happiness, so that is her name. Happiness.

Felicidad, in Spanish. Hortelano's English was poor, but he knew that much. An absurdly optimistic name, under the circumstances. He hoped it would help her on the rough road ahead.

In the morning, when the banks unlocked their doors, he went to his branch and opened an account in the child's name. Happiness Akpan—he'd got the surname from the mother's medical chart. He didn't quite believe what he was doing. He deposited a hundred euros and clutched the passbook in his hand as he left. Happiness's parents would possess this tiny crack in the wall that was Europe, this evidence, perhaps, of their intent to become law-abiding citizens. He wouldn't tell Luisa, of course.

But when he went back in the afternoon the mother wasn't there. The nurse on duty, fidgeting, pretended to be studying something on her computer screen. No, the woman hadn't been taken to the detention camp.

−She's an illegal! *Coño!* How the hell'd she get out?

She'd walked out, apparently. With the baby, during the night. It had been with her for feeding.

−We're not her jailers, *capitán*. A senior nurse, her tone somewhere between apologetic and defiant, had joined the other at the desk. −We're understaffed, you know, since the cutbacks. We can't be constantly checking.

Perhaps she'd had help from some sympathetic orderly, a fellow countryman, a former migrant. Even planned it with her husband, the day he'd been brought to see her, though the chances of *him* escaping were small. Flee into the countryside with her child, find some hidden migrant camp; god knew there were enough of them. Fury bit into Hortelano as he stood there holding the passbook, anger at *them*, their ingratitude, their stupidity. How could she risk her health like that, her child's?

Yet if it had been him and Luisa, he'd have done the same thing. He threw the passbook on the desk and walked out, only to go back half an hour later, shamefaced, to retrieve it.

The next day was his day off. He wandered for miles through the streets, bearing a melancholy he couldn't shake, and stopped for a coffee and brandy late in the afternoon in a bar in a mostly north African neighbourhood. The gutturality of Arabic wound round him, men hunched over their games of chess and backgammon, strenuously not looking at him. Even out of uniform he was a type—casual polo shirt, hair cut short, his air of authority, of self-possession. The spreading warmth of a second brandy restored him, but only a little. He might as well have *POLICÍA* tattooed on his forehead. Wherever Adebayo and Olabisi and Happiness had gone, no one was going to tell *him*.

He had to go to Madrid for a meeting of SEMAR heads of station. At two-fifteen in the morning his cellphone rang. Luisa, sobbing hysterically. All he could make out was Felipe, Felipe. It was Marisol who took the phone, who said with a kind of urgent calm –He had an accident, Papá, we're going to the hospital right now, we don't know anything, we'll call you.

He dressed with one hand, phoned Carmona, the head of the Sección de Tráfico back home. Carmona phoned back an-eternity-that-might-have-been-five-minutes later. *Está bien, su hijo, está bien, pero malherido.* He's okay, your son — Hortelano breathed again for the first time in centuries—but he's badly injured. A crushed leg, the paramedic had said, nose probably broken, concussion. A drunk driver, some British expat, had hit the Renault head on. Felipe hadn't been wearing a seatbelt. The others in the car, Felipe's girlfriend Luz and another couple, had only minor injuries.

–*Gracias, muchísimas gracias, hombre. ¿Se lo agradezco, se lo agradezco un montón, entiende?* Grateful, incredibly grateful: such paltry words. Sobs erupted from somewhere in his stomach and he bent over, still clutching the phone, tears sliding down the screen.

∅

Felipe was ridiculously fine. Had come round from the concussion and was already telling self-deprecating jokes from his hospital bed. It was the rest of the family who were a mess—Luisa shaking visibly, Marisol clutching her old teddy bear, Emilia (summoned from her teaching job in Ronda) furious. None of this would have happened if Felipe had gone home when he was supposed to, hadn't missed his curfew.

—If only you'd grounded him the last time, she kept saying. —That's what you'd have done with me. Why's it different for boys?

Marisol had flung herself at her father when he came in and he had to gently disengage from her before leaning over the bed. —*Hola, chaval. ¿Qué hostias es eso?*

Felipe's unconquerable grin hadn't changed despite the blackened and puffed-up eyes, the wad of bandages across the bridge of his nose. *Hey, Papá. Look what I had to do to get you to come home.* At eighteen you were invulnerable, of course. It could have been so different. A wet night, the roads slick with rain, the boy was staggeringly lucky, considering the state of the car. One of the paramedics had phoned him, no doubt on Carmona's instructions, said it looked like an accordion.

Outside he and Luisa and Emilia spoke to the doctor. A set of ligaments in the right knee—he couldn't, afterwards, remember the medical term—had been severed when the car keys were driven in. A very common injury in such cases, the doctor said. The boy's right foot had been forced up by the accelerator pedal, the metatarsal bones pushed sideways, several toe bones crushed. There would be surgeries, a long recovery. Yes, of course, he'd walk again, even run again, though squats might be difficult. He was young, healthy, he'd heal rapidly.

    –Stupid, stupid, stupid, said Emilia when the doctor had gone, flinging her hands in the air, turning on her parents. –Why weren't you paying attention?

It was forty-eight hours later before he remembered about the Nigerian family. This time he called Victoria Beltrán Sokol at the Centro de Refugiados. The last time they'd met was at some local government meeting about dealing with migrants. –You haven't changed, you Guardia, she'd told him afterwards, shouldering a hefty briefcase. –You think you've been rehabilitated, but your minds haven't. Especially you old ones.

    Her insult had stung him into rudeness. –Keep helping them and how many do you think we'll have here? A million? Two? Five? They take advantage of people like you.

    –And you, how do you suppose *you* got here? Some Berber way back fucked some Christian girl when they invaded, and twelve hundred years later you're the result. Her high heels went snapping out of the meeting room before he could think of an answer.

    Now, on the phone, he said –It's Hortelano. The cop. You know, the one with that Berber ancestor who fucked a Christian.

    He could have sworn she was smiling, but her voice was cool. –To what do I owe the pleasure?

    –I'm acting in a civilian capacity. You can believe me or not. I'm looking for a Nigerian couple with a newborn baby. They left the Hospital Santa Catarina last Thursday.

—I wouldn't tell you even if I knew. You know that.

—I opened a bank account in the baby's name. Can I leave the passbook with you?

A silence on the other end, either stunned or wary. At last she said —Is this some new kind of snare you've come up with?

—*¡Dios mío, mujer!* Does it sound like one to you? Once you have the passbook you can check with the bank yourself.

Another silence. —All right. But don't come here in person. Even as a civilian. You'll scare people off. Is there someone you can send instead?

There was only Marisol, since he wasn't about to let Luisa in on what he'd done. He needed a document delivered over on the other side of town, could she drop it off when she went to her cousin's on Friday? She and Lola were about the same age and close.

His brother-in-law drove Marisol home just before midnight, in a Guardia car this time, he must have just got off shift. —You should have told me, she said, letting her school bag drop to the floor. Through the window Diego gave a brief wave before driving off.

—Tell you what, *chiquita*?

—I opened it, I wanted to see. Uncle Diego says—

—You *showed* it to him?

—He says it's illegal, what you're doing. He says you ought to be careful.

He grabbed her, more roughly than he'd intended. —Where's it now, *coño*? She cried out and wrenched herself from his grip and stood glaring at him.

–Don't worry, I took it to the Centro. Your precious little black baby. You never opened a bank account for *me*— She broke off in tears and ran upstairs.

He sat for hours, or so it seemed, with his head in his hands. What was the matter with him? Taking a stupid risk like that—did he *want* to be caught? Retire before you hate your uniform, his old staff sergeant Berenguer had told him back when he was still a young sergeant. But he didn't hate, and besides at fifty-four he was too young to retire. Didn't love his pistol more than his wife, either, despite what Luisa might think. Out of the group of six friends who'd gone through basic training together, two were dead—one to suicide—and three divorced. He was the only one still married to the same woman.

He woke partway through the night, muscles nagging, having fallen asleep on the sofa. Olabisi stood there in the dark, her face gleaming in a stray band of light from a streetlamp. She held Happiness in the crook of her arm, the passbook in her hand. –Thank you, she said, softly, in English. –When she grow up, I tell her about you. About money from heaven. She pressed the passbook to her chest, and disappeared.

It was stress, his doctor told him—a new one, young, young enough to be his son. He'd been working too hard, and what with the business with Felipe—well, it wasn't surprising.

–Take a week off, relax, the doctor said, handing him a note. –Bet you don't know how, do you, *capitán*?

Which wasn't quite true. He dutifully took two weeks in the summer, went with Luisa to London or Paris, though he checked his phone for calls from Arregui when she wasn't looking. While she shopped at Liberty's or Galeries Lafayette he wandered through the amphibian and reptile collections in the natural history museums, becoming again that small boy with a net and a jam jar in the marshes of the Guadalquivir estuary.

The first day off he slept in, met Luisa in town for lunch and afterwards visited Felipe, who shot down the ward in a wheelchair, tipped back on the wheels and spun himself round.

–You've been here too long, Hortelano told him, and cuffed him lightly on the head.

–How about a jailbreak, Papá?

–Maybe I can take you out for an hour. I'll check with the nurse.

At a nearby bar, where Hortelano wrestled the chair over the narrow doorsill, Felipe ordered a beer and a plate of his favourite *pinchos morunos*. Food and drink, noisy vibrant life—things Felipe, and he himself, took for granted. He'd drop in to the nearest church that evening, maybe even go to mass. Light a candle of gratitude for his son's survival. He hadn't felt such pleasure watching the boy eat since Felipe was a baby.

The church held perhaps a dozen people, mostly old, for the seven o'clock mass. No one he knew—other than, occasionally, Luisa—went to church anymore, except at Christmas and Easter. Still, he found himself automatically murmuring the old responses, and afterwards, leaving the church, stopped to speak to the priest.

–My boy was in a car accident, came through okay. He felt embarrassed, caught out. –We've lived in the neighbourhood for years.

The priest nodded, face lit with understanding. Hortelano felt even smaller. God, he remembered, too late, was a sneaky bugger who figured out exactly how to prick your conscience.

–Come again, the priest said. –Bring the boy when he's well enough. It was an invitation, not an admonition. Hortelano liked the priest's young face, his firm and slightly sweaty grip. Where were the corpulent ones of his youth, bringing down their stinging paddles on his palms?

Victoria emailed him three days later. Could they meet somewhere? She had something to tell him. He chose the north African bar on the edge of town, no one would know him there. She arrived in jeans and a sweatshirt and track shoes, not the suits she wore to court. Hair surprisingly dishevelled. He was momentarily aroused.

–We've found them, your Nigerians.

–Where? He surprised himself with his urgency.

–Let's just say they're safe for the time being. She twisted an unruly curl behind an ear. –We're launching an action to have the baby declared a Spanish citizen. The lawyer thinks we have a plausible case.

Was this why she'd emailed? Simply to let him know, to put his mind at rest? It seemed unlikely. Or maybe she was softening, too. The baby's influence was remarkable.

–If you said you'd be willing to employ Olabisi as a domestic, it would increase her chances.

He stared dumbly at her, flung his arms out, exasperated. –You know I can't.

–You opened that account, remember? She straightened, though she still came only to his shoulder. –Or are you chickening out?

He'd had to pull strings, of course. Victoria would know

that. The name was obviously foreign, and he'd had no ID for the child.

—I've done what I could. More than I should have, in fact.

—If you hired Olabisi, you'd see the baby every day.

Was she being deliberately disingenuous? Behind her dark glasses he couldn't read her expression.

—I could have you brought into the station. Charged with assisting illegals. Carries a six-year sentence, as you know.

—We could have you subpoenaed.

—Give me a break, Victoria, all right? My plate's full these days. My son was injured a couple of weeks back.

—Yes, I heard. Car accident. With a *British* immigrant. She pushed her glasses up on her head, met his gaze and held it. —All life's an ongoing accident, hadn't you heard? Only for some people more than others.

There was a weight on his chest. Some days it was lighter and some heavier. Felipe came home, his old self except for the crutches, but the weight didn't change. Hortelano went back to his doctor, who sent him for a battery of tests that revealed nothing.

—You've got the blood pressure of a teenager, Enrique. Low cholesterol, healthy weight, excellent stamina—what's the matter, you don't live on coffee like the rest of them? Describe the pain again for me.

It wasn't a pain but a heaviness, bearing down on him. At night sometimes he woke sweating, unable to breathe. At other times—he might just be walking down the street, taking a phone call—it had shape and movement and warmth. That was when it was most unbearable, when he wanted to tear his chest open and extract it, whatever it was. He had trouble swallowing, and for no reason he could fathom the smell of fresh bread made him gag. He went out of his way to avoid *panaderías*, and made excuses if Luisa asked him to pick up a baguette on weekend mornings.

At the physiotherapy clinic Felipe was working on the flexion of his right knee; the surgeon had talked of further surgery if it didn't loosen up. Hortelano picked him up after one such session, the boy's face reddened and sweaty. Felipe slid into the passenger seat and lay back, breathing hard, eyes closed.

—It hurts, Papá.

—*Te oigo, hombre.* Let's go for a drive. Up in the hills.

They drove north out of the city, as though they were heading for the A-45 and the Alpujarran village where Enrique had spent his summers when his grandmother was still alive. He hadn't been here in years, not since he was a young officer and hadn't yet learned to leave the work behind. Stunted pine trees and gorse grew among the rocks and scrub. Below them, as the road climbed, the Mediterranean dwindled to a blue river. He opened the window, letting in the crisp air, the whistling chatter of a nightingale.

—Wow! What a drop! Felipe leaned across his father to peer over the edge. —I could bring the bike up here, it'd be a fantastic ride down.

—Sure. Wipe out and wreck the other knee. Your poor mother.

Felipe, his head now thrust out his own window, either didn't hear or chose to ignore him. —What's that up there, Papá?

The remains of a shepherd hut, perhaps, a tumble of broken stones. Hortelano slowed the car. A movement caught their eye on the hillside above—two men in hooded jackets who almost immediately slipped into the trees.

–¡*Joder!* Felipe said, still staring out the window. –It's illegal migrants, isn't it?

Hortelano pulled over and parked. –Let's find out.

They climbed slowly up through the scrub, Felipe limping awkwardly with his cane. Crickets clicked around them in the silence. Tucked among the trees near the top were scraps of plastic and cardboard and tin sheeting. A gaggle of children had gathered, two or three of them standing with thumbs in mouths. A thread of dirty smoke rose from a fire somewhere.

–What are you going to do, Papá? Arrest them?

His heart was hammering, as if from the climb, his mouth was dry, and that weight moved in his chest again. He wasn't in uniform—he'd changed at the clinic—but he always carried his ID.

–I don't know. Now keep quiet, all right?

A man who might have been Moroccan or Algerian was coming toward them, a scarf wrapped round his head. He held out a piece of paper, which turned out to be an employment contract. Agrupa Costera, S.L.—one of the companies growing tomatoes and cucumbers under those kilometres of plastic sheeting along the coast. Some of that sheeting must have made its way up here. The man watched, on edge, as Hortelano studied the document.

–No place to live down there. He flapped his hand at the curve of beach far below them, the white glitter of yachts. His eyes moved from Hortelano to Felipe and back again.

–I'm looking for a woman from Nigeria. Hortelano pulled out his badge. –Olabisi Akpan. She has a baby.

–No black people here. The man spread his hands, nervous, placating. –All here from Maroc, Tunisie, Algérie.

–Is there another camp near here?

–Lots of camps, the man said eagerly — too eagerly, perhaps. –Black people camps, many different camps. He folded the contract with precision and tucked it in an inside pocket. Perhaps he was the only one with a job, sent out as a decoy on behalf of all those who didn't, who would never have one. Hortelano could go and check, of course. But that meant knowledge he'd have to act on.

–What was that about, Papá? Felipe said on their way back to the car. –Who's the woman you're looking for?

–Someone Arregui asked me to check on. The lie came fluently, easily. –She left the hospital she was in. Just disappeared.

–*¡Joder!* Felipe said again, more softly. He looked suddenly older than his age, burdened by something unexpected. –Living like that. It's crazy. You want me to drive, Papá?

–Just give me a moment, *hijo*. The breathlessness took him by surprise; in the car he sat with his eyes closed. Maybe it was a tumour, a belated punishment for all those years of smoking. Surely only such a thing — blackened, malignant, triumphant — could feel like this, could take on a life of its own.

When they got home Luisa met them at the door, her whole being radiant. –*¡Qué te parece, noticias maravillosas!* Emilia had phoned half an hour ago. They were going to be grandparents.

It was Diego, a folded newspaper in his hand, who brought the news. Hortelano, working on his monthly report, half-rose, surprised to see him here at headquarters, but Diego had already flung the paper on his desk.

—Take a look. Page five.

Baby Born at Sea Gains Citizenship. Above the article a photo of Olabisi with her head down, hurrying out of a doorway, the baby a swaddled bundle in her arms, and just behind her a woman in a tailored suit who must be the lawyer. *Olabisi Comfort Akpan and daughter Happiness, aged four months, leaving judge's chambers,* read the caption. Hortelano scanned the article. The granting of citizenship didn't include the father, who was to be deported the following week.

—That's her, isn't it? An upper lip flickered as Diego tilted his chin. —The one you were helping out?

—I got her a bank account. As you know. That's all.

—And then you went on stress leave. Diego, moving to the window, stood looking out at the port. —None of my business, Kiko, but maybe it's getting too much for you.

Susana had been telling Diego that for years, ever since that botched robbery when a bullet caught her husband in the thigh. Hortelano was thankful Luisa wasn't as high-strung as her sister. He refolded the newspaper.

—Heart palpitations, that's all. The doctor says I'm fine. I've had all the tests.

—They say when you take it home you've been here too long. Diego turned from the window and regarded him. —And you're taking it home, Kiko. That risk you took, when you sent Marisol—He made a face. Hortelano laughed, not very convincingly.

—It got to me, that business with the baby. *¿Normal, no?* Look, did Susana tell you our news?

—You're changing the subject. Diego paused at the desk on his way out, punched Hortelano's shoulder. —It gets in here — he pointed to his chest — and you're done for. Wasn't it just last year Alamillo over in Contraband died of a heart attack?

He phoned Victoria during a lull that evening, after most of the day shift had gone home. Probably, like him, she often worked late. Her voice at the other end of the line was hoarse with what might have been weariness. —So you saw the story.

—What's she going to do now?

—Stay here. Try sponsoring her husband a few years down the road. He wants that, too.

To lose everything you'd known in order to survive, you and your child. He tried, and failed, to imagine it.

—Can I see her?

—What for?

He wouldn't be able to explain the weight in his chest, the simple need to see the baby again. In Ronda, not so very far away, his grandchild swam in its mother's belly, warm and safe. Olabisi must have parents who would never see their granddaughter. What was that proverb his grandmother had been fond of quoting? *Take care of your patch of dirt because it tells you who you are.* Much of his grandparents' village had been expropriated to make way for the new freeway that saved you forty-five minutes between Granada and Seville. Now all his friends, where they could, were buying up ruined houses in their family villages, trying to rebuild what was.

—Will you give her a letter, if I write one?

An outbreath of exasperation on the other end of the line. –She doesn't read Spanish.

–It's for her daughter. When she grows up she'll be able to read it.

–Sure, okay, whatever. Mail it to me. The receiver clicked at the other end.

He hadn't known either of his grandfathers. His grandfather on his father's side — Enrique was named after him — had been a teacher in a small Asturian village, a gentle, patient man who his son, Enrique's father, barely remembered. He'd been shot during the Civil War for being a supporter of the Republicans, aged thirty-one. His killer was a member of the Guardia Civil stationed in the same village. The killer had died in his sleep, years later; the two families had lived side by side in the village for years. Enrique's father had gone to school with the killer's son. Everyone in the village knew the truth, but nobody talked about it. Sometimes Enrique wondered what his grandfather would have thought about him being in the Guardia. Sometimes he wondered why his own father — a taciturn businessman he'd never been close to — hadn't avenged the death himself.

His other grandfather, his mother's father, had died of cancer soon after Enrique was born. A stubborn, opinionated man with a quick temper who'd been mayor of his tiny Alpujarran village for years and maintained an elaborate enmity with the local priest over the perfidy of the Church. Had belonged to an anarcho-syndicalist trade union until he'd lost his leg on some construction job. Enrique's mother, a small girl at the end of the Civil War, remembered how her father had hidden fleeing Republican soldiers in the rafters of the village's olive press. And from the village's dim Moorish past there were stories of a Christian siege when the villagers had survived for six months on rats and rancid olives and at the end burned their own houses rather than let them be taken.

So as a grandparent he had no role models, except by hearsay. Still, he supposed he'd figure it out. He'd been a father, after all, and hoped he hadn't botched the job too badly.

He took his time on it. Began and ripped up a dozen versions. In the end he remembered that Pilar—Meléndez—had taken a picture of him that afternoon on her cellphone, his vest bulging with human flesh. He scrolled through his email. In the crook of his arms the baby's eyes were wide, a puzzled crease on her forehead. He could feel her weight again, her pulsing warmth, the silk of her baby skin. He printed the photo out and wrote his name on the back, along with the date, and after some hesitation added his badge number and the name of his station. Someday she might want to get in touch with him. He was sure she'd be able to track him down. He couldn't think of anything to say in a letter that wasn't banal or obvious or self-serving.

She stood beside him at the sink that night when he went for a glass of water. She was tall, graceful, plump-armed, in her twenties perhaps, dressed like any smart young Spanish woman. She watched him as he drank and he expected her to say something, but she didn't. Somehow he knew that Olabisi was dead and that the father—Adebayo, was that his name?—had never returned. The light from the streetlamp outside gleamed along the curve of Happiness's cheek like a blessing.

Nicolás Enrique Alarcón Hortelano was born on July 23rd, weight 3.7 kilograms, with his mother's green-hazel eyes and his grandfather's stubborn chin, or so Enrique flattered himself. For the second time in less than a year he found himself visiting a maternity ward, only this time he wore his uniform, taking off his cap as he leaned over his grandson where he lay in the hospital bassinet. *Hola, chavalito*, he said softly, tears starting, and blew his nose discreetly. He hadn't felt so limp, so vulnerable, since Nicolás's mother had been born all those years ago—was it really twenty-seven? What happened to time that it could stretch and shrink in such fashion? He thought of Happiness and wondered if, years from now, the two of them, she and Nicolás, would meet. Perhaps they'd end up at school together, who knew. Even lovers, or married, in a new Spain where such unions were taken for granted. It wasn't something he wished for, but it might be what the future demanded of him.

–*Ouf*, a boy, he said teasingly to Emilia that afternoon, taking his turn in a mob of visitors. –Make sure he keeps his curfews, won't you. Though I'm sure he'll be much better behaved than Felipe.

Emilia was flushed, triumphant, Nicolás asleep on her stomach, tiny mouth half-open. –He's an oldest child, everybody'll be strict with him, she shot back. –The middle child gets away with everything.

–Better not have a middle, then.

—Ah, we only want two. That avoids the problem, doesn't it? She bent her head and nuzzled the baby's cheek. —Besides, he'll have an *abuelo* who's a cop to keep him in line.

They celebrated Felipe's nineteenth birthday and the baby's *bautismo* on a dazzling August day in a restaurant noted for its pork loin in brandy, Enrique's favourite dish. Nicolás was passed from hand to hand like a parcel, ending up at last asleep on Luisa's practised lap. Enrique gave an impromptu speech—something about parenthood and how you couldn't prepare for it, though afterwards he couldn't remember what he'd said.

—You're definitely getting soft, Papá, Felipe said, nudging him while Luz bent gurglingly over the baby. Quiet, steadfast Luz, with the same ready smile as Luisa. They'd be married before long, Felipe and Luz, or perhaps it was just that he approved of her. Not like Marisol's boyfriend, an offhand seventeen-year-old in a leather motorcycle jacket who reminded him so much of his younger self he wanted to slug him. But then he hadn't much liked Emilia's husband, Roberto, at first—a stolid lump of a man, or so he'd seemed, who did something obscure in computer software at the university—though watching him now, gazing at his baby son with a kind of tender amazement, Enrique remembered how he'd felt watching his own first-born, and his throat seized up. They slit you open, children. Made you helpless with tenderness, and then gnawed you to death.

He hadn't felt that thing in his chest for months but here it was, weighing him down with its melancholy even in the midst of celebration. That night, getting up yet again to piss, he half-expected to see Olabisi or Happiness, but instead, incomprehensibly, it was a teenage Nicolás who stood before him. Cocky, self-possessed, full of life — just the way he himself had been at that age. The boy spoke to him in what sounded like Arabic, and for a moment he wasn't sure it was Nicolás after all. But it was all there in his body — his mother's eyes, his father's dark curls, something of his uncle Felipe's slouching grace. And something else, something almost feline that reminded him a little of Luisa when he'd first met her, slightly aloof, as though there was something being held back, some secret that couldn't be told.

They spent a week in a villa on the Atlantic coast, a vacation gift to the new parents from Roberto's family. Each morning Enrique carried Nicolás down to the beach so he could absorb the sound of the waves. They sat together in a canvas beach chair, he and the child, while families picnicked on the sand around them. Luisa claimed he was far more enamoured than he'd been with his own children, which he didn't dispute. From time to time he adjusted the baby's blanket or tilted the miniature sunhat farther over his eyes. Sometimes, unless Nicolás began whimpering for a feeding first, he sat until Emilia came to find him, accusing him, mockingly, of kidnapping her son.

In the baby's face he sometimes saw his own, and sometimes Luisa's, sometimes even Felipe's or Marisol's. The baby had gathered them all up and held them in his small fists. That was what babies were for — he'd never realized. They inherited nothing, they built from scratch, but they already knew how to clutch and squeeze and hold on. They were dangerous, in fact. Little terrorists of the heart. His wife must have known that all along, but he hadn't. It was a pity, really, it had taken him so long to learn.

When Emilia came they were both asleep, the man and the child. She lifted Nicolás out of her father's arms and held him up to the sky. *—Pillín*, she whispered, Little rascal. Little king. She drew the floppy hat down over her father's face so he could sleep on, undisturbed.

THE GATE OF CHARITY

When the young woman came up the hill on the donkey Lalla was indoors, shredding cilantro with her fingers. From the window she saw first the man, holding the donkey's bridle, and then the woman, swaying woozily. She poured a glass of *citron pressé* from the jugful she'd made that morning and ran outside. —Put on your headscarf, shameless one, her mother called after her.

The man was helping the woman dismount while the children crowded round, staring, mesmerized. Foreigners rarely came here; it wasn't on the standard tour company routes. Lalla waded through, holding the glass high. The woman, pale from the heat, was shrinking back from the clutching children.

—Here, Lalla said in English, holding the glass out. —It's lemonade. Good. But sip slowly.

The woman took the glass hesitantly and pressed it to her forehead, then drank in gulps. Lalla grabbed her wrist to slow her down. —I'm Lalla. Lalla Tanzir. You must join us for lunch. Her quick glance included the man, too.

–Thank you, you are too kind. His Arabic was almost accentless, his gestures those of a native. –I am Henri and this is Cathérine, he added, using the French versions of their names, perhaps to show off his fluency, his knowledge of the country, though neither of them looked French. American, perhaps — at least the woman. Were they lovers, or simply travelling together? The woman wore a wedding ring but the man didn't.

–She doesn't look well. You'd better bring her inside.

They put the woman, Lalla and her mother, in her mother's bedroom, kept dark and cool by the drawn shutters and the thick walls. –It's the elevation, Lalla told her. –You aren't used to it. Her mother brought a damp cloth to lay across the woman's forehead. –Just rest, Lalla said. –You'll feel better by evening.

The man, Henri, sat under a fig tree with the other men: Lalla's grandfather, her brother Firhun, the Hasnaoui boys. There were no men of working age left, only the old, the young, the crippled. She and her mother carried out trays of *harira*, olives, a goat tagine, followed by dates and oranges and mint tea. The man Henri ate like a native, dipping his fingers unselfconsciously in the couscous. She didn't know why but there was something she didn't trust about him. Did his eyes rest a little too long on Firhun, on the younger of the Hasnaouis? She'd met men like him at the hotel, foreigners who rarely spoke Arabic the way he did but who slipped the maître d' folded bills and asked in whispers where boys could be found.

Afterwards, while the men talked, she and her mother ate their own meal in the kitchen. Only a spoonful remained of the tagine, her favourite dish, though since her grandmother's death no one could make it the way she had. Familiar fury flared for an instant. In Fez, with her friends, they neither ate last, after the men and children, nor wore headscarves. Of the five of them only Zahra had a fiancé. Najia was studying to be a dental hygienist; Mernissa planned to join her aunt, who owned her own restaurant, in America; Amina volunteered at a centre for unmarried mothers. The Qur'an, as Zahra often pointed out, spoke of the equality of men and women; hadn't the Prophet himself, peace be upon him, taught women and ordered that they be allowed to attend the mosques at night? Hadn't he said, "If any do deeds of righteousness be they male or female and have faith, they will enter Heaven, and not the least injustice will be done to them?"

In practice women were lesser, were ignored and silenced. It was precisely why Lalla had left her village at seventeen, to her parents' despair. Her brother Yunes had left the year before, as all the young men did, a fact lamented but accepted as some harsh and inexplicable fate. —I bore children only to give them away, her mother said, mouth twisted in bitterness, the day Lalla left.

But when her father fell ill, and could no longer farm their small plot of land, and then died, it was Lalla's earnings that kept the family going. Each month, standing in the bank queue to send the money, she was quickened by an emboldening pride, a fierce, self-reliant joy. Pride was a defect of character, so the Qur'an said, but why shouldn't she feel proud to be supporting her mother and her grandfather and her three younger brothers?

—Riuza's daughter is to be married in the autumn, her mother said, peeling an orange with strong thick nails. —To think the two of you played together just yesterday!

Riuza and her mother were cousins. She would have to

come back for the wedding, which meant asking for more time off, though she and Jedira barely talked anymore. She helped herself to another date and spat out her annoyance along with the stone.

–And there's been little rain again this year, it's getting harder and harder to find pasture.

Her mother did not comment on the visitors. Why they —why anyone—might want to wander the earth in such a fashion was an insoluble mystery, and ultimately of no interest. She rose, poured a little water into a basin, and rinsed her fingers. –Go and see if the men want more tea. And don't linger talking. That may be how you behave in the city, but here we still respect our traditions.

It was in Fez, her first day at the hotel, where she learned that such traditions were not, in fact, as unbreakable as stone. She'd heard rumours, of course, but had never before seen such things with her own eyes. Foreign women came and went as they pleased, alone. They arrived alone too, suitcases haloed with the dust and glory of airports in distant countries. Men talked to them, laughed with them, flirted with them, yet the sky did not fall. That was also the day that Mouna, one of the chambermaids, went down to the kitchen and brought back a tall glass of pale yellow liquid in which cubes of glass floated. No, not glass—ice. How could it exist on such a hot day? It was magic, a piece of magic she brought home a few years later, buying a generator for the village and then a tiny fridge for her parents' home. The *citron pressé* recipe, too, though her mother refused to touch the stuff.

—City softness, she said, waving her hand dismissively.
—For women who sit around and do nothing all day.

Lalla tried to point out that she herself, living in a city,
worked hard, but her mother just stared at her. —You speak
to the people who come to the hotel, you give them rooms!
How is that hard? Making that disapproving *tzut* sound
against the roof of her mouth.

Her mother would never understand how the city was
like a crouching cheetah, ready to pounce. At first the speed
and confusion and crush of people had been bewildering.
Lalla, who in the hills could read the sign of rabbit and
jackal, could name all the stars and constellations—*Dhat
al-Kursi*, the Enthroned, *Fam al-Hut*, the Mouth of the
Fish—here stepped into the path of traffic, blundered everywhere with her country manners. Though surely persistence
and politeness as she walked the streets, knocking on doors,
would bring what she wanted?

By then, in her squalid room in the medina, she was thin
and desperate, living on bruised fruit, stale *khobz*. It was an
appeal to a relative, a distant cousin she'd never met, that
saved her. The cousin owed her grandfather on her father's
side a favour, never repaid, and knew a wealthy politician
whose wife's family part-owned a hotel. The letter he sent,
like the ice, turned out to be a magic talisman, bestowing
what had seemed unreachable. In the hotel she marvelled
at the softness of the sheets, the television in each room,
the inlaid furniture. The few pieces in her own home,
dragged from one mountain village to another when her
grandmother married, were scarred and antiquated. Each
scar carried a story, all of which she would inherit, like the
pair of earrings in filigreed gold given to her by her mother

when she began to bleed. Her first act when she arrived in Fez was to sell them. Along with the coins, tinkling one by one into her palms, she heard the distant sound of rent clothing, the ululations of grief.

By evening the woman said she felt better. Lalla sat outside with her, away from the men, who were smoking and telling jokes beneath the fig tree. The woman turned out to be Canadian, not American. Perhaps from the French part of the country, with that name, though she spoke no French. Grey eyes, tanned skin, brown hair cropped stylishly short — she might have passed, perhaps, for a European, except for the gestures, the way she moved her body. She was puzzled by Lalla's green eyes. Not uncommon in the Rifi villages, Lalla told her.

–Teach me some Berber, the woman said.

–Not Berber, Tamazight. Lalla refilled her glass with mint tea, keeping her voice neutral. –Berber is what the Romans called us. Barbarians.

–Tamazight, she repeated, mangling it. –How do you say, *I'm looking for a boy from these villages*? Can you write it down?

–Why? Why are you looking for a boy?

–I found his body. On a beach in Spain. The woman looked off into the distance where the hills were indigo shadows. –I wanted to let his family know what happened to him.

For a moment Lalla's heart clutched. But no, the boy had some sort of tattoo on his ankle, which Yunes most certainly had not had and would never have agreed to.

–Why? If he's not a relative?

Cathérine stared at her. —I thought how they must feel, not knowing. How *I* would feel. It seemed like a — well, like an obligation.

—So it's for you. *You* want to feel better. Scorn turned her voice harsh; foreign women could indulge every silly little whim. —You want to feel pure and noble.

Cathérine blinked as though Lalla had hit her.

—I was on holiday when I — when he spoke to me on that beach. I had a fight with my husband to come here.

Ah, the missing husband, of whom the only trace was the woman's ring. She and the man were lovers after all. Would have met after she'd arrived. Perhaps he liked women as well as boys.

—You left your husband in Canada to come all the way here? And after Cathérine had explained —He was jealous, then, Lalla said, that you were interested in this other man. She jerked her head at the group under the tree, silhouettes in the darkness.

—No, no, not that. He thought it was a waste of time, my looking. He went back to Spain.

And this woman believed that? Believed that men, and especially husbands, always told the truth? The moon, an antique coin, rose above them. —Are you cold? Lalla said. —Would you like a shawl?

—You're very kind. Cathérine got up, slowly, leaning on Lalla's shoulder for support. —I think I'll go back to bed. I think that would be best.

In the morning they went from house to house, Lalla explaining, Cathérine holding out the sheet of paper, now torn and faded. In each house, as Lalla could have told her, the answer was the same. No one knew of such a boy, though the villages had sacrificed many boys to the Bab al-Zakat, the Gate of Charity, the strait that lay between their own country and that richer continent to the north. They proposed names simply as offerings, as opportunities to say them aloud so that Allah himself might bless them, wherever they were.

–Pick a boy, any boy, Lalla said. –Go to Spain or France or Germany and find him.

But of course the woman would not do that. Dedicating one's life to such a pursuit would be—well, madness. The kind of thing only a saint would do. –You are named for a Christian saint, aren't you? Lalla asked. She'd learned her first English from an elderly priest who had retired in Morocco and spent a summer in the village, working as a translator with some archeological dig, long abandoned.

It was as her father said: Christians, unlike Muslims, observed their religion only on Sundays. The woman was explaining that her grandmother had gone on pilgrimages, that she herself was on a kind of pilgrimage.

–My own brother disappeared in Europe, Lalla said, glancing down; a spider had run across her sandal. –My father thinks he took up with some European woman. I think he drowned, like the rest of them. Or maybe he's living in one of those camps. She had seen these on TV but had not told her mother. Such an ending was worse than death; it brought nothing but shame. –Mostly, now, I don't think about it. It only makes me sad. Sad and angry.

Firhun came up then, swaggering a little. The man of the house, with his father and older brother gone, he was performing for the benefit of the foreign woman. –American?

he said, one of the few English words he knew, and gave his heartbreaking smile. —Look, I dance for you!

Lalla gave him a push that almost sent him sprawling, adding in their own language —Get lost, monkey. Firhun gave an exaggerated moue of despair and sauntered off. —Now *he* wants to go, too, Lalla said. —English, she added bitterly, the language of the drowned, though Cathérine had walked ahead and didn't hear her.

The last house was Riuza's. She, too, had lost a firstborn son to that ravenous continent, though so long ago that Lalla didn't remember him. Riuza took a framed photograph from an alcove, pressed it against her breasts, then held it out to Cathérine. The boy in the frame looked even younger than Firhun, with soft, almost feminine eyes and a thin face too serious for its years. —My first fruit, my lovely boy, Riuza said, kissing the cold lips. —My only child from my first marriage. I lost him when he was seventeen. He's thirty-seven now, if he's still alive, *insh'allah*. Have you seen him? Do you know him?

Riuza was not deterred by the fact, pointed out by Lalla, of Europe's millions. —You take, you take, she said, thrusting the photograph at Cathérine. She gestured vigorously at Lalla. —She can find him, my Ahmed, no? You tell her I have a little money, I'll pay. Better to look for a live boy than a dead one, no?

Ahmed, like Yunes, like hundreds of others, was keeping the fish and the seaweed company at the bottom of the Mediterranean. Lalla laid her hand gently on Riuza's arm. —Keep your photograph, Riuza. Bring it to the wedding. To Cathérine, who looked as though she was going to dissolve, she said —Don't you dare take him on. Go home. Find your husband.

They walked back through the village in the blistering heat. Lalla swept her arm across the dry brown hills below them. −You see, don't you? That there's nothing here? She looked at Cathérine with a kind of disgusted envy. −And here you are, looking for a man who doesn't belong to you! I can't even afford to look for my own brother.

Henri was leaning against the tree, smoking, when they returned. Cathérine wiped her face with her scarf, said something about the heat, and went indoors. Henri ground out his cigarette in the dirt and took Lalla aside. −Well? Did she learn anything?

−Of course not. Lalla shook his hand off; hadn't it lingered a little too long? −You knew that when you brought her here.

−I learned long ago that I know nothing in this country. Henri watched her levelly, his arms folded. −I thought there was a possibility. She was desperate.

−You *encouraged* her.

Finding the boy's family would make her feel needed. Would make both of them, Cathérine and the man, feel needed. He sat down heavily in one of the rickety deck chairs she'd scrounged from the hotel. It was hard to tell how old he was — probably in his fifties, though he was fit and lean.

−If it had been *your* brother, wouldn't you have been relieved? He ran a hand through hair too blond to be natural. −She wanted to help.

More than once, walking down a Fez street, Lalla had seen him, just a glimpse, getting out of a taxi, buying something at a stall. Her big brother, two years older, the one who'd carried her up and down on his back playing at donkey and rider. It was Yunes, so her mother said, who had rescued his two-year-old sister when she'd fallen into the stream that ran at the bottom of the hill. It was her turn, now, to carry Yunes. She'd been carrying him for eight years.

—If you found his family, was she going to sleep with you? She used the crude Arabic for *fuck*.

Henri stared at her and then away, across the hills, and she felt the briefest moment of shame. —She was blundering around pointlessly. She needed someone who knew the ropes.

—Lalla! It was her mother's voice through the window, sharp, irritated. In the kitchen steam rose from a pot, a bowl of lemons sat on the table. —Here. Her mother waved a knife at her. —Work for a change, shameless one, instead of idling in gossip. Through idle words the devil slips in sideways.

The devil stuck his pitchfork into her all through lunch, showering fiery little sparks, though she didn't know why. There was something, something... Perhaps they were simply here to buy kif and taking elaborate precautions. Or could the man be a paid informant for some European police unit investigating smuggling? The woman Cathérine was putty in anyone's hands, that much was clear. Were they working together, and the story of the husband was just a ruse?

After lunch, Henri asleep in his chair outside, she went to the house of the Hasnaouis, where he was spending his nights. —The foreigner sent me here, she told Darifa Hasnaoui when she opened the door. —He needs something from his room.

His room had been offered by Darifa and her husband, now sleeping in their sons' room while the boys slept on

87

blankets in the kitchen. Lalla hunted swiftly through a faded blue knapsack leaning against the wall, a pair of jeans hanging over a chair. Only a wallet that held what appeared to be a legitimate driver's licence, bearing the name *Henk de Ruiter*, a street address in Tangier, a date of birth: March 23, 1972. That made him forty-nine. There was nothing else to explain who he was, though the Moroccan flavour of his Arabic meant he'd lived here a long time. A wad of notes in dirhams had been stuffed under the mattress, but whether it was his or the Hasnaouis' she didn't know. She picked up the jeans again, sniffed the pockets for the scent of kif. Before she put the wallet back, a last rooting yielded a photo, wedged behind the driver's licence. A young man, perhaps in his early twenties, dark-eyed, heavy-lidded, a sensual lower lip. Probably Moroccan, definitely Maghrebi. But so what? What was that to her? Perhaps Henri's protestations about Cathérine were genuine after all.

–It's not here, she told Darifa, what he sent me for. Perhaps he lost it.

Darifa offered tea and they sat drinking in the shade, backs absorbing the heat from the house's walls. –Do you remember, Darifa said, that time we decided to take the goats out?

They'd gone early one morning, without permission, two girls of nine and thirteen. Darifa, promised in marriage the following year, was rebelling, but it had really all been Lalla's idea. What did the boys do all day, out with the goats? Lay in the sunshine, wandered the hills, while she and Darifa and the other girls sweated in the kitchens beside their mothers. It was even harder, in her own case, since she had no sisters to share chores with. Of course they were punished when they got back — Darifa beaten, Lalla condemned to limited food and silence for a week—but oh, the day they'd had! The tiny waterfall where they ate lunch, a patch of rare pale-lemon narcissus, a cave that echoed away into darkness and where they dared each other to go deeper. On their way out, near the entrance, Lalla found the scattered blue beads of a necklace. –A couple must have come here to—you know, Darifa said, wide-eyed, and broke into nervous giggles. –Like what the male goat does to the female. To make babies!

Why anyone would want to make babies—they were heavy, they cried all the time, they were always dirtying themselves—Lalla had no idea. Darifa must be wrong. No woman would come here with any man but her husband, and why would they need to hide? She and Darifa collected the beads, divided them between them, and promised eternal friendship.

–You must marry among us, her mother said often, which meant a Rifi man, but where was she going to find one when they'd all gone to Europe? There had been two or three love affairs, brief ones, in Fez, though of course she did not tell her mother that. Besides, did it count if your heart was still intact?

–And who, she always retorted, am I to marry? Darifa's crazy uncle? Or Jedira's brother—you want him as a son-in-law? The brother had come back after five years in Germany, lamed, impoverished. No one knew what had happened— he no longer spoke.

Her mother shook a ladle at her. –May the wrath of Allah descend upon your impertinence! Know this—marry a Fassi and I won't come to your wedding.

Which wasn't true. It only meant that her mother wanted her to live in the village, to lead the life that generations of women before them had lived, a dim caravan stretching into some misty past. A life that was no longer possible, at least not for her. Lalla, transplanted elsewhere, was rooting herself in different ground. Her grandfather, deaf and mostly silent, had startled her once by saying –When a woman leaves a village for the city, she leaves them all. Was *them* her family, or the entire Rif? Or both?

–Is there a man? Darifa asked over the tea. –You can tell me. My lips are sealed.

Darifa, her old friend of the blue beads, had married at fourteen, had her first child nine months later. Had borne two sons, thereby guaranteeing the family honour, then a stillborn daughter, and just last year a third son, who slept in a cradle in the cool of the kitchen. Lalla was twenty-four and still single. Darifa admired her but, Lalla knew, did not envy. A woman of her age without a husband, much less a child!

–And you, she said to Darifa, can tell me what you think of the foreigner. What he's doing here with the woman.

–Mezwar and I talked before he went out to the field this morning. Mezwar says it's obvious — he likes boys. Anyone can tell, Mezwar says. Maybe the woman hired him as a guide.

But he had touched her, Lalla, in a way that had made the heat rise in her face, as though he'd crawled inside her. Did he like boys *and* girls? What was in it for him, that he'd brought a foreign woman to this out-of-the-way place, knowing it was a waste of time?

–You think so? Darifa said, as wide-eyed as she had been at thirteen, only now it was Lalla leading the way. –Could a man be so confused about what he likes? She considered for a moment. –Or perhaps he's practising, the way the male kid goats do, mounting each other. She smothered a giggle behind her hand. —Only a foreigner could practise so long without getting it right.

In the evening the woman did not appear for dinner. Henri borrowed a flashlight and went off exploring on his own. Lalla sat with the other women by the fountain, where the generator powered a single streetlight. The talk today was of Jedira's wedding to a widower of forty in a village fifty kilometres away; she would have two young stepchildren. Also of the planting—the tomatoes, the onions, the alfalfa —and the weather: always the weather, the portents in the sky. One or two of the women sat with the latest letter from son or brother or husband in their laps, but no one asked questions. It was bad manners and moreover dangerous. The evil eye might notice the one spoken of, so far away, so unprotected, and take revenge.

In the morning Cathérine was running a fever, burning up between the bed's thin sheets. Lalla's mother bathed her hands and face with rosewater while the Hasnaoui boys and Firhun walked the three kilometres to the next village to get the doctor. Not a real doctor—a medical student whose family had run out of money for his studies. For the twentieth time Lalla walked among the houses with her cellphone, trying and failing to get a signal. Firhun and the Hasnaoui boys came back not with the medical student, who was away, but with the midwife, the *qabla*, who knew the efficacy of touch and herbs and charmed sayings. Lalla, who in Fez had discovered the spotless white of doctors' clinics, the power of those framed credentials on the walls, made a face but said nothing. The midwife was ushered into her mother's bedroom and stayed there a long time.

–Perhaps it will help, Henri said, smoking again and staring up at the brassy sky. –The best medicine, when one gets sick, is that produced by the place, I've discovered. When I had bronchitis I went to a herbalist in Tangier.

That was what foreigners always did: succumbed to whatever, to them, was exotic. Lalla had cleaned foreigners' shit from toilets, had stripped beds that still stank of their lovemaking, and knew that exotic was a thing of the mind, not an actual destination.

–Then you were lucky. My aunt in another village died in childbirth because there was no doctor. Who knows what's in those herbs?

But no doubt he was right. The woman Cathérine was under a spell. She would get better because she believed. –You should take her away from here, Lalla said sharply. –Take her out of Africa. This place doesn't agree with her.

Henri said nothing, merely watched a buzzard circling overhead as though around some invisible pole. Lalla went back inside with the cellphone. Her mother always looked at it as though it might suddenly leap up and seize her by the throat. *That thing*, she called it, or, *That demon-mirror*. She had once seen her face in the darkened screen and been genuinely frightened.

In Lalla's small apartment in Fez — two rooms, really, in what had once been a sprawling family home — she gave no quarter to demons, especially those invented to control women. Twice, early on, daring herself, she'd brought a man to this apartment. With the first she'd held hands and kissed, both of them too inexperienced, too shy, to go further. The second had been rougher, had grabbed her and shoved her on the bed. When she wouldn't take her clothes off he had slapped her, hard, across the face, had screamed abuse at her and left. The sting of his slap still dwelt there, in her cheek, a part of its tissues and cells. These days she chose somewhere she could run from: a darkened doorway, a disused building, where they could rub up against each other hungrily, explore with hands and tongues. She'd done everything with a man except allow his penis inside her. Her friends — except for Zahra, who said she was waiting till marriage, to the others' laughter — had all done the same.

—Why are you saving yourself? Najia teased. —Do you think *they* are? More laughter.

—And you, when you're betrothed, Zahra said, looking round fiercely at them, will all head off to the nearest clinic to have your — she gestured at her crotch — to have *that* restored.

—*I* won't, said Amina, emphatic. —Because I'm not planning to marry. Mernissa isn't either. Or Najia, or Lalla. They looked at each other and then away, affecting blasé, bored expressions. —Why would anyone get married anyway? No offence, Zahra, your Muhammad's a lovely boy, but *really*.

In her inmost self Lalla was sure this was only bravado, except for her. The others would succumb, eventually, to their parents' pressure, their family's scorn, but she would work forever at the Hôtel Zalagh, become a manager some day, perhaps even run the place. A life of catering to others, yes, but at least you were paid for it, unlike living in your husband's village and trying to please your in-laws. Not to mention having babies one after the other. Here was a way of living, hitherto unimagined, where in her free time no one told her what she must do or where she must go. She could not, now, go back to being blind and deaf.

The midwife left the room only to eat a quick bowl of *harira*. The foreign woman was delirious, raving—she believed she could see the boy. Lalla went and stood in the doorway, watching her mother hovering over the bed. —Azemmur, Cathérine muttered, over and over again. What did that mean? It wasn't a person's name. What did an olive tree have to do with anything?

—Cathérine. Lalla shooed her mother out and leaned over the bed, took her damp hand. —Cathérine, can you hear me?

Cathérine opened her eyes, focus drifting from Lalla's face to a far corner of the room. —Bourdoud, she said, Bouazzoun. So that was it—she was remembering place names, perhaps the names of towns she'd been to or intended to visit, looking for the boy.

—You're here in the village, with us, Lalla said firmly, and shook her shoulder. Cathérine looked at her as though she was trying to decipher Lalla's English. —You're not well. You have a fever.

—He chose me, Cathérine said. —He's relying on me. She turned her eyes to the window as if she saw him there. Lalla couldn't help it; she followed Cathérine's gaze. And could have sworn she saw something, some shadow, move across the shutters. She ran and pulled them open, but there was no one there, only a woman climbing the hill from the fountain with her bucket.

—Why would he choose you, of all people? she said,

turning to shut out whatever Cathérine thought she saw. It was preposterous, such a claim. But Cathérine had closed her eyes and did not answer. Lalla's mother and the midwife came back in then, bustling, purposeful, and Lalla slipped out. The room smelled of stale sheets and sweat; she was glad to escape.

Firhun wanted his English lesson. –*How are you? I am fine*, he repeated after her as they sat round the table outside. Her younger brothers Tabat and Kenan leaned on her shoulders, staring at the textbook she'd bought in Fez. It came with a CD so Firhun could practise when she wasn't there. –*Fine, fine, fine*! sang the youngest until she slapped him. He pretended to fall to the ground, clutching his arm in exaggerated pain.

–I need other words, Firhun said, annoyed. –For when they're being pests. He swung at Tabat, who leapt deftly out of reach.

–Just concentrate. I'll ask the questions, you answer. *How are you?*

–*I am fine.*

–*Would you like a drink?*

–*Yes, a coffee, please.* He pronounced it *pliz*. Lalla corrected him and had him repeat it.

Her mother came out into the courtyard, frowning.

–Firhun. I need you. Now.

–Only because she doesn't want me practising, Firhun said in an undertone, standing up and slouching after his mother into the house.

–*Would you like a drink?* Kenan said. He was a good mimic; he had a better ear than Firhun. –*Yes, a coffee, please*

—answering himself. —It's my turn, Lalla. Teach me, teach me.

She sat holding the heavy textbook. This was the way of the world, wasn't it? Who was she to stop them? For a searing moment Kenan lay lifeless on a beach somewhere on the Spanish coast. How would she feel then? Her father wasn't alive to blame her, but she would blame herself. *I bore children only to give them away.*

She was supposed to return to Fez the next day, but her mother and the midwife would not want Henri in the room, and anyway he knew no Tamazight. Why had Cathérine come blundering into their lives, ruining everything, dragging that strange man in her wake? Lalla would wait another day; that was all. She was due on shift at the hotel desk; she couldn't afford to take more time off.

She sat outside in the shade against the wall, turning the collar on one of Tabat's shirts to hide the wear while her mother napped indoors. —My eyes aren't what they used to be, she'd said the evening before, trying to sew in lamplight, and for the first time Lalla understood that her mother, at forty-five, was old. Women of that age in Fez, at least the well-off ones, were still trim, still desirable. With her drooping breasts, her bulging stomach—seven pregnancies in fourteen years, including two miscarriages—her mother looked twenty years older. What would happen when she died? Would Tabat and Kenan have left by then, too? In which case there'd be no one to uphold the Tanzir name in the village, to honour the Tanzir dead.

Her grandfather had spoken of how his father and uncles fought the French and Spanish on behalf of the Rif

Republic in the 1920s. She'd grown up hearing the stories of how they'd massacred thirteen thousand Spanish troops at Anoual. One day, *insh'allah*, their leader, 'Abd al-Karim, would come back from exile to avenge them, though he'd been dead for nearly fifty years. One of the uncles — Lalla couldn't remember which — had died within a week from the mustard gas the Spanish had dropped from their planes, his body a mass of yellow blisters. Two others had died of cancer in their fifties. It was common knowledge that many fields in the Rif were still contaminated.

Under the fig tree Henri was talking to her brothers about Germany, about Holland. Phrases floated her way: *three and a half million people in Berlin now...ride past the canals on your bicycle...yes, many young men like you speak English...* Would their Dutch or German wives know how to turn the collars of their shirts? She stabbed her needle into the fabric, her jaw tightening.

—Don't believe him! she called out loudly. —Don't believe everything he says!

—What do *you* know? Tabat called back. —You've never been there.

It didn't matter what he said or how he said it; her brothers would take it all in without question. Especially Firhun — he was such a romantic. He'd argued with their father about what had happened to Yunes. Of course Yunes wouldn't desert them like that. He only wanted to surprise them, to come back with his pockets spilling money. Even now, Lalla was sure, Firhun expected Yunes to swing into the village any day, perhaps at the wheel of some new American car.

—But I hear stories, she called back, which was true. Some of the hotel staff had worked in Europe. All the Germans knew how to do was make money, her boss, Ghanim, said.

Told her of being spat at, called a dirty Arab. The Rifi people were not Arab, of course, they were Amazighen, but the Germans didn't know the difference.

–Of course there are others, many others, who are kind, Ghanim added, but never in a million years will you be German. Even your kids will not be German.

After her brothers tired of tales of paradise and ran off to find their friends, Henri came to join her. Lalla laid her sewing down on her lap and accepted a cigarette.

–You shouldn't tell them such things. Encourage them.

–Why not? There's nothing for them here.

–Have you been there lately? Not for years, I'd bet. What are you doing here, anyway? She looked at him closely, but behind his sunglasses his expression was unreadable.

–Living. Living more fully, that is. Life is a risk or it is nothing. In Germany… He pressed his fingers against the bridge of his nose, in irritation perhaps, his glasses riding up. –But for your brothers—it's better than this, isn't it? Do they have other choices?

–They can do what I did. Go to Fez, look for work.

But even as she said it she knew it wasn't true. The cities were full of the uneducated, the unemployed. You might find work as a labourer but it paid nothing. Firhun and Tabat and Kenan were bright, especially Firhun, but university was as distant as the moon.

–I'm useful here, Henri added without prompting. –Useful in a number of different ways.

–You're a spy, then. An informer.

He took off his glasses and stared at her with his pale blue eyes. –What have I done? Why don't you like me? He leaned toward her and touched her hand, though this time she felt nothing. Had she imagined it before?

–I chose your country. I chose it over mine, thirty years ago. Believe me, I've no desire to be thrown out.

By evening the fever had broken. Lalla didn't know if the herbs were responsible and didn't care. Cathérine and the man needed to be got rid of as soon as possible. Perhaps the swirls of unease and excitement they had stirred up would settle down, once they were gone. Cathérine was actually able to sit up and eat a little soup.

–You must thank your mother for me, she's been so kind, she told Lalla, her voice slow, laboured. –And the other woman, too. She asked for her purse and drew out dirham notes, but Lalla wouldn't take them.

–You were ill, were we going to refuse you? Of course not. It's unthinkable.

Cathérine's eyes filled and she took Lalla's hand. –Do you see? she said, pointing to the shutters. –Do you see, there?

Did she still think she saw the boy?

–*There*. It's a sort of glowing.

–It's the sun. It's setting, Lalla said impatiently.

–But *within* that. Can't you see it? What a pity. They all come back, you see. So Azemmur says.

–She knows, that one, Lalla's grandfather said as Lalla and her mother served the evening meal. Henri was eating with the Hasnaouis; Darifa said he was picking up some words, he had a quick ear. It was almost ten o'clock, vivid streaks of light still visible in the west. A moth butted clumsily against the metal lampshade that hung above them.

—Which one, grandfather? Lalla said patiently, humouring him. Much of the time he was a boy again, bringing down birds with his slingshot, running barefoot across the hillsides.

—The foreign woman. A rare thing, for a foreigner to see.

Lalla and her mother exchanged glances. —Allah chooses whom He will, the grandfather murmured, his fingers coated with couscous. —My sister saw. Also my mother. I've told you these things, mother of Yunes.

—Yes, you have, Lalla's mother said briskly. —Now eat up, while it's hot.

He'd taken to wandering, she told Lalla later as they washed the dishes. —Riuza's father did that, too; she had to tie him to a chair. I'm so afraid he'll fall and we won't be able to find him.

Later, getting ready for bed, Lalla saw her grandfather standing outside, staring at something. Was he lost in his mind again? When she went to urge him to come inside, he pointed at the window of the room where Cathérine lay. —It was there a moment ago. It's gone now.

—What, grandfather?

He glanced at her with an amused, pitying smile. —You live in the city now. No one in the city sees these things. Those big lights — he spread his hands wide — blot out everything.

Cathérine and Henri left the following morning, just before Lalla's taxi arrived. She'd suggested they ride with her, but Henk insisted on returning the donkey to its owner. They moved down the hill and out of sight, Cathérine swaying unsteadily on the donkey's back.

Lalla sat with her back against the house wall, smoking. The taxi would take her to the main road; from there she could catch the bus that went to Fez. She'd be in the city, the city with its cries of muezzins and street vendors, its packed sidewalk cafés, its minarets and wide French streets, by early evening. It was home now, not this dusty little place, though the smell of lavender through a doorway changed her instantly into a nine-year-old again, helping her mother hang sprigs in the sleeping rooms as protection against bad dreams. Her mother had sent a cloth pouch of it with Cathérine, the same pouches embroidered with symbols that lay between the underthings in the dresser in her own apartment.

A biologist staying at the hotel once had told her that lavender was antibacterial. It was even used to help cypress trees grow in the High Atlas. He'd come to Morocco as part of a study financed by his own university to find out why.

THE OUD-MAKER'S SON

He lay half-asleep among the wood shavings of his father's workshop. The sound of the file lulled him as his father fitted the ribs for the bowl, planed the wood for the peg box. The clop of donkeys' hooves filtered in from the street, the bells of the water vendors. His father had promised him an oud of his own for his next birthday. For lessons he would send him to the famous blind oud player in Rue Sidi Boujida, where people gathered at the doorway to listen, sipping mint tea in silence. A thin beam of sunlight struck his cheek and he nuzzled deeper into the fragrant shavings. His mother was calling him but he'd stay here forever...

Law du 'ā' al-kalb yustajāb, kān bitishtī al-dunyā'izām. If the prayers of dogs were answered, bones would rain from the sky.

He sat up abruptly, heart juddering. Where was he? He pressed the heels of his hands to his temples. He was sitting in a study carrel, sunlight flooding a window, other students at nearby tables whispering together in twos and threes. The library at the university, of course. Where he was supposed to be studying for tomorrow's exam.

Except that, for the third time this week, the voices had returned.

They'd disappeared so long ago he'd forgotten about them. The voices—sometimes it was just one voice—spoke in a language he didn't understand. Sometimes they were staticky, as if a frequency wasn't tuned in. As a child he'd repeated what they said to his mother, who laughed, and then frowned, and then scolded, and then ignored. As he grew older they came less often, and eventually they went away.

He stood up and tried to shake himself free. Perhaps ignoring them was the answer. Otherwise it was a kind of possession, which frightened him. How could something like this happen to someone in the twenty-first century? To *him*, of all people—Nicolás Alarcón Hortelano, someone who believed in reason and precision, in the beauty and formality of mathematics. Numbers were predictable; they behaved. Tame lions, with him holding the whip, leaping through hoops at his command.

Núria was stirring soup and Maite was setting the table when he opened the door. The light in the hall was out, something to do with the switch—the landlord had been promising to fix it for months.

—Abuelito's coming to eat with us. Núria took soup bowls from a cupboard, not looking at him. —Now don't start any arguments, okay?

—More stories about the Guardia, then, he said resignedly, dropping his pack on the floor as Núria gave an irritated shrug. He'd never understood why his grandfather had joined up, though his little brother lapped up the tales. Nowadays the Guardia had a new official name — Protectores de la Patria — and sweeping powers to arrest anyone they deemed a threat to the state. On campus they patrolled in their black uniforms, visors on their black helmets pulled down, rifles at the ready. The head of the PP — the students called them *las putas de la patria*, the whores of the state — was known to be the real leader of the government, paralyzed and squabbling since the Crash eleven years ago. His uncle Felipe was a deputy with the government for the province of Seville, and he didn't understand that, either. His grandfather didn't talk about Felipe.

Daniel, sitting in the living room's one good chair, was watching his InScreen — Nicolás could tell by the glazed look in his eyes — even though he was only allowed to for an hour after dinner. Nicolás cuffed him, none too gently, on the side of the head, and Daniel sheepishly tapped the tiny chrome implant in his ear. Apart from addiction problems the InScreen was expensive. They couldn't afford another bill like last month's.

The doorbell rang and Daniel tore off to answer it. The elderly man who stood there, erect, whitehaired, swung Daniel upward as if he was still small instead of eight years old. *–¿Qué tal, chavalito?* he said, grinning, and to Nicolás *–Hola, grandote.* He always called Nicolás that because of his height. *–¿Qué va los estudios?* And Nicolás, murmuring automatically that his courses were going well, thanks, heard a phrase in that strange language erupt in his head. For the first time he understood its meaning: *One should not contradict the words of old men.*

∅

Those nightmares about drowning, for example—was that where things had started? Enrique couldn't remember for certain, only that Emilia had come to him in tears when Nicolás was just a toddler, wanting to know what was wrong with her child, how had he and Mamá handled such things? The truth was they hadn't had to, though he didn't say that to Emilia. Nicolás hadn't been two before he was waking at night screaming and had to be held for hours. *The boat, it's sinking*, he sobbed, or *Save us, please save us!* No one knew what to make of it. The child had never been on a boat. Emilia had the idea of taking him to swimming lessons, but he'd screamed there, too, and refused to go in the pool.

Then there'd been the business of food. He loved couscous, Emilia reported, and would have eaten it at every meal if she'd let him. He refused absolutely to touch pork. The summer he was three she found him sitting in the garden, clutching a sprig of mint. *Make Abuelita some mint tea*, he'd insisted, *Abuelita would like some tea*—only it wasn't true, Luisa didn't like the taste. There were the things he couldn't have known, too, like the fields of lavender he'd seen on TV at about the same age. *Alhucema*, he said, startling everybody with his use of the word. *Ras el hanout*, he added, and kept repeating the phrase insistently until Emilia wrote it down phonetically and checked it in an online dictionary. Ras el hanout, it turned out, was a Moroccan spice containing lavender. Emilia bought some at the supermarket and made it into a paste for roast chicken, which Nicolás ate with gusto, though Núria, then a year old, wouldn't touch it.

–Tell us again, Abuelito. Tell us the one about the burglar and how the police dog found him.

They were drinking coffee after dinner, mixed with chicory to make it go further (an old trick of his great-great-grandmother's during the Civil War, so Nicolás had heard).

–Not again, *chiquitín*! You can't want that one again!

It was an old formula, this pulling and pushing, begging and denying. Made the story all the sweeter, Nicolás supposed, remembering that he'd done it too at Daniel's age. Daniel was going to be a vet, he told everyone, or a dog trainer. He'd join the Guardia— the Protectores— just like Abuelo and look after the police dogs. Nicolás hoped fervently this wouldn't happen.

–Well, there was a robbery on the Gran Via in Madrid, the famous Grassy jewellery store— it's not there anymore — and Lobo and his handler were called in. A big black German shepherd, fierce and courageous—

The door opened and their mother came in, carrying her briefcase and looking exhausted as usual. –*¡Ay Dios mío*, what a day! She tossed the briefcase in a corner and kicked her heels off. –First one of the girls slaps another, and then there's a free-for-all in the middle of the classroom, imagine, and then there's a bomb scare—

–Mamá, Mamá, Abuelito's telling a story and you interrupted!

And because it was her baby, her little pet, Danielito, their mother crooned at him and cradled his head against her breasts and said *pues claro*, her own story could wait, Abuelo should continue and it wouldn't be the story about Lobo, would it?

— and Lobo leapt through the door they'd blown off and seized the burglar by the arm and he was so scared he peed his pants—shrieks of laughter from Daniel—and the cops threw him in the paddy wagon and took him off to jail.

–What happened to Lobo, Abuelito?

–Well, he got old, eventually, and retired, like all police officers, and went to live with his handler until he died. I'm sure Lobo's great-great-grandsons are working with the Guardia today.

Something tore at Nicolás's chest—a brief glimpse of himself sitting outside somewhere with his arms round a scrawny dog, a puppy really, golden and gangly, and his mother calling him in that strange language that remained just out of reach. The glimpse vanished, throwing him almost physically back in his chair. He smelled thyme and jasmine, felt hot sandy soil under his bare feet, the rough fur of the puppy. He was having trouble breathing and hoped no one had noticed. His asthma attacks, his mother had called them when he was young.

His phone rang, sparing him. Kassim, one of his co-workers at his restaurant job, wanting him to fill in for some-one else who'd called in sick. –*Ciao, todos*, he said, grabbing his jacket and leaping through the door before anyone could ask where he was going.

Whatever it was the boy would outgrow it, or so the doctor told them. Emilia clung to his words as if they were scripture, though Enrique's aunt—the boy's great-great-aunt—said it was obvious the boy was psychic and that no one outgrew that. –It's a gift and a curse, the great-aunt said. –But it's given, not chosen.

Village superstition, Enrique told himself, and repeated none of it to Emilia. But the words lingered, troubling him.

Madness ran in his mother's family, so he'd been told—a great-uncle had been confined to a mental institution. And yet most of the time Nico was simply an ordinary boy, bright, lively, prone to mischief. Enrique went so far as to consult a psychiatrist friend of his, who said it was likely the boy had peculiarly vivid dreams and was too young, yet, to be able to separate them from reality. When, some time later, the boy's father lashed out at him for his lies, Enrique took him aside. –Look, Roberto. They're dreams, that's all. Vivid dreams. That's what a doctor friend of mine told me.

–But he's almost six! He knows the difference between dreams and reality!

For his seventh birthday Nicolás asked for, and received, an oud, and still remembered the look of relief on his mother's face when it turned out he didn't already know how to play it. He slept with it next to him and sometimes talked to it. Lay with his hands resting on its pear-shaped belly, smelling again the fragrance of the wood shavings, hearing the sounds from the street, his father's voice. It was the only thing that calmed him, that reassured him everything was all right.

And then, as the doctor had predicted, the dreams—if that was what they were—faded away. When the boy's parents separated—Nico was thirteen—Enrique watched him guardedly, wondering if stress would trigger something, but saw nothing. In fact the boy seemed unusually mature for his age, serious and responsible, perhaps because he was the eldest and now had to be man of the house before he was ready. He was thoughtful and tender with his sisters, though impatient with Daniel, who admittedly was a handful. For a while Enrique wondered if Daniel had inherited the same condition—he had seen his grandmother, he told everyone just after Luisa died of that stroke, sitting on the sofa, watching them all and smiling—but there were no further visitations.

Nicolás was at the restaurant setting tables when the distant banging of pots and pans started. Some demo or other, then; he'd lost track. In high school he'd gone to them all, had even joined the EUFD, Students United for a Different Future—then it had been EUCF, Students United Against the Future—but now he didn't care anymore. What was one more demo going to achieve? The truth was that survival itself was a full-time job. He'd got his part-time one the only way possible, through the cousin of a friend. People made do through bartering, scrounging, living with their families. The only hope was to emigrate. Robberies had gone up twenty-fold, or so he'd heard.

   —¡*Venga, hombre!* It was a friend from his mathematics class, Miguel, thrusting his head through the door. —Everybody's in the street, everybody, you wouldn't believe. He raced off before Nicolás could answer. Nicolás flung down the napkins and followed slowly—the restaurant was empty anyway. As he neared the plaza he could hear the roar and heave of the crowd, the chanting of slogans. Two young women rushed past pushing toddlers in strollers. A heavyset man, sweating in the heat, was urging people onward to the square through a megaphone.

   Nicolás leaned against a wall at one of the square's entrances, watching. They could shout themselves hoarse, they could dent every pan and pot in the country; nothing would change. He was about to go back to the restaurant when he heard the first screams, the first crump of tear gas rounds.

Someone near him yelled for a medic as a middle-aged man collapsed. Then mounted police were charging the square in several directions, and the women he'd seen earlier with the strollers rushed past him again. He didn't hesitate but turned and ran after them. *Cobarde*, a voice whispered inside him. *Cobarde.*

Ahead of him another young woman tripped on the pavement and went down. Dark hair pulled back in a pony-tail, a distinctive red jacket—it was Paola, wasn't it, she was in one of his classes. He grabbed her arm and helped her up and they limped onward. From behind him came the hammer of running feet, the clatter of police shields. The door to some shop opened, children's toys in its window, and a stout older woman waved them frantically inside. There, among the stuffed animals and the building blocks, they watched the demonstrators race past, followed by the police.

–*Cabrones*, the woman muttered, though Nicolás wasn't sure who she meant. –Where's it all going to end, I ask you? What hope is there?

She guided Paola into the back office, propped her swollen ankle up on a chair, and fetched a cold cloth as a compress. –I don't take sides here, she said. –It's a nasty business all round, no? And everyone loses, everyone.

Once things had quietened Nicolás helped Paola walk to the restaurant. Strands of tear gas still floated in the street, people hurried past with eyes averted. Outside the restaurant chairs and tables had been overturned, but otherwise the place was undamaged. A man from the grocery shop opposite was sweeping up glass.

–Are you hungry? Nicolás asked, unlocking the door. –There's some *pescado frito* left from lunch.

–Fish? Real fish?

Nicolás grimaced. —The fake stuff, of course. But there's lots of it.

Paola limped to a chair. —There's still fish in Germany. Or so I hear.

—That's where you're going? He fetched a bottle of wine and poured glasses for both of them.

—That's why I switched to engineering. There's jobs there, my cousin got one last year. My parents have already gone back to Italy, to Milan.

So that explained the faint accent. Her mouth was too big for beauty but there was something about the glossy hair escaping from its elastic, the cut of the red jacket, that suggested ease and comfort.

She shifted position and winced and bent to touch her ankle. —And you, what are you going to do?

Nicolás shrugged. —Go to America, maybe. I have a friend there.

The truth was he didn't know a soul in America and couldn't have left his mother and siblings on their own anyway, but this smooth assured girl irritated him. What made her think she had any more control of the future?

—How come you were at the demo? He refilled her glass.

—Oh, I wasn't. She laughed and the bluish-grey eyes lit up. —I was just walking past. The eyes narrowed reflectively. —I had no idea. It was horrible.

—I'll take you home, he said, but she shook her head and took out her cellphone.

—I can take a taxi. If my sister-in-law can't come and get me.

No one he knew took taxis. —My brother's a businessman, Paola said — airily, or so it seemed. —He says there's talk about a coalition, the PDN and that new party.

That was what his uncle had said the month before, over the obligatory Easter dinner at his beautiful house in Seville. They were in talks, he and the other members of the Partido Democrático Nuevo, the centrist party, with the new upstart, the one that had done so well in the last regional elections, the far-right New Dawn.

—So now we're in bed with the fascists, Nicolás had said as his mother and his aunt Marisol exchanged glances. —No one I know even voted in the last elections.

—They're not like the old fascists, his uncle said tartly. —They're realists, they understand how things work. Don't you think we need a government?

—A government that'll make things better, yes, but those thugs—

—Nicolás, his mother said, raising her eyebrows warningly, but by then he had the bit between his teeth and didn't care.

—Do you know how people are living, Tío— *real* people? They don't have Mercedes and trips to New York like you. Their children don't go to boarding school in Switzerland. Haven't you noticed? They have nothing. Just like us.

That night, when they returned home, he had to go and lie down in his bedroom, holding the oud. He hadn't taken it out of its case since he could remember. He gently blew the dust off and held it close, trying to hear again those sounds, those voices, only this time they spoke to him not of the safety of his father's workshop but of danger and menace. He understood, without knowing how, that secular music was now forbidden and his father no longer made ouds, ever since gunmen had burst into the workshop and destroyed his instruments. He bent over the oud. There, at the base of the pear-shaped bowl, was a tiny crack, one he'd never noticed before. He tightened his arms round the instrument and closed his eyes.

It was Núria, of all people, who told him about the Enrejado, the Lattice, starting up in their own neighbourhood. He'd heard about the Lattices that threaded across the country and, increasingly, the continent, forming their own trading and banking and schooling networks, but he hadn't paid much attention. Now here was his sixteen-year-old sister getting involved in some dubious organization.

—Rafael says we'll never have a government, Núria said as they cleaned up the kitchen together. —Rafael says it's a thing of the past, vertical organizations.

—Who's Rafael?

—He's a shop steward at the electronics repair place near here.

—I don't think you should get involved. It isn't safe.

—And it's safe if I *don't* get involved? Besides, it's too late. I'm helping with the bread run. She flung her hair back. —After what you said to uncle Felipe, I thought you'd be pleased.

The bread run, it turned out, was a distribution system, to which the neighbourhood bakeries contributed free bread each morning for the poorest households. —We're starting to organize other things, too. Soap and canned food and milk and—oh, all kinds of stuff. Daniel came with me last time.

He saw them, his sister and brother, lying bloodied on a street somewhere, clouds of tear gas encircling them. —Leave Daniel out of this, he said, grabbing her arm, but she pushed back.

−Who do you think you are? Papá? Anyway it's too late. Daniel's got his own little run, right in this street.

In this new, cracked world, one where the voices were leaking in again, he was helpless. But at least if he joined the Lattice he could keep an eye on Núria and Daniel. Even Maite, who'd just turned thirteen, was on some computer committee or other. −And on Friday nights there's concerts in the square by the church. All the local musicians come.

−Why didn't you tell me before?

Núria regarded him pityingly. −With your head full of mathematics? Admit it, Nicolás, you live in your own world most of the time.

−Suppose I want to help?

−Then you can teach math. We have classes for anyone who wants to come.

He went reluctantly, sure no one would turn up, but instead there were sixteen people, including Rafael from the electronics place — the heavyset man he'd seen at the demo — who'd always wanted to learn calculus. Afterwards Rafael took him aside. −We need more teachers, you know, for other subjects. Bring your friends. And money to buy supplies. If you know anyone who has any.

The next time he saw Paola in class he told her about the Lattice. −You ought to organize one in your own neighbourhood.

−But no one there needs free bread, she said, puzzled. Her ankle was still bandaged but she didn't seem to be limping anymore.

−We need sympathizers, Nicolás said. −We need money and support. It's your job to find it. What about that brother of yours, the businessman? Start with him.

Ø

The violence, according to Kassim, was the sign of a system in its death throes, flailing like a wounded beast. That was how it had been in Algeria during the Civil War of the nineties, when Kassim's father, a journalist, had been assassinated, and his mother had fled with her two-year-old son and his sisters to Spain. Now Kassim worked for the university newspaper, writing a column called The State Is Not Your Friend.

–Western democracies were supposed to be different, he told Nicolás. –In Algeria we have a saying: *If you step on its paw, even the tamest cheetah bares its teeth.*

Nicolás brought him to the neighbourhood to teach classes in journalism and media. Paola, to everyone's surprise, came by too, bringing a large donation of cash. Her brother had been very grateful for her rescue at the demo, she told Nicolás, handing over the neatly folded wad of bills. –He wants me to leave, to join our parents in Italy. He says things are going to get much worse.

–He's right, Kassim said. They were sitting on the steps of the church, waiting for the Friday night concert to start. –But there's nowhere to run. You think Italy's better off?

Paola said something that was drowned out by the sounds of a guitar tuning up. –You have to stand your ground somewhere, Kassim added. –Your brother won't be able to protect you forever. His teeth, white in the fading light, looked positively feral; Nicolás decided he wouldn't want Kassim as an enemy.

Paola came regularly after that to the concerts, often bringing food to contribute to the weekly feast that Núria and the other women organized. She even sat in on the strategy meetings organized by Rafael and Kassim and a group of workers from a local furniture factory. They called themselves the Grupo Cinco de Junio, in honour of a day the previous year when police on horseback, charging a group of demonstrators, had killed three. Nicolás watched with skepticism, especially when Paola and Kassim began sleeping together.

—Raising her consciousness, are you? he teased Kassim, who grinned and shrugged.

—*Hombre*, everyone's capable of change. That demo — that's what started it. When your own body feels the impact... He shrugged again. —You should come. There's big plans afoot.

Instead Nicolás went home and raised his own barricade, one made out of elegant formulas, necklace-like strings of numbers. Someday the world would come to its senses and his knowledge would be needed in the rebuilding. There was probably a mathematical formula for what had gone wrong, and another formula that would correct it, except that his own skills weren't yet equal to finding the solution.

In July a general strike was called. Once again Nicolás locked the door of the restaurant and joined the tens of thousands in the city's central plaza, more out of concern for Núria and Daniel than anything else. Nevertheless he sang and shouted slogans along with the others until he was hoarse, until the sun went down and the police on horseback appeared. At one point he thought he saw Paola in the distance, but when he craned his neck she'd disappeared. Kassim was at the microphone, exhorting everyone, even housewives, to join the strike when the police charged. In the melee that followed, Nicolás saw only that Kassim, dragged off the platform by his hair, was one of the first arrested and taken to the waiting police vans. Despite the refrain in his head about his own cowardice he slipped away round a corner and didn't stop until he reached home.

He shut himself in his bedroom and took out the oud. The hairline crack had widened; he could see the inside of the oud's belly through it. He touched it with his fingers and thought he heard his father's voice — saddened, hesitant — murmuring something in that unknown language.

He joined the crowds outside the prison, taking with him a change of clothes, food, and a few books. He was Kassim's cousin, bringing vital medication, he told the guards, and though they looked at him suspiciously they let him in. Kassim, brought to the other side of a tiny grille, was still in the filthy and bloodied jeans he'd been arrested in, a deep gash over one eye. When he saw Nicolás he narrowed his eyes.

–What are you doing here?

–Bringing you these. Nicolás handed over the items for inspection by the guards. –Is there anything else you need?

–A lawyer. As soon as possible. How's Paola?

In truth he didn't know; apart from that possible glimpse at the demo, he hadn't seen her in days.

–Tell her to stay out of all this. She'll only get hurt.

As if to confirm what he said a woman's scream arose from somewhere in the distance, followed by what sounded like a body being flung against the wall.

–This isn't a revolution, Kassim said, dropping his voice to a whisper. –It's a war. Oh, and an InScreen, too. Figure out a way to smuggle one in.

He slept with his face on the stones of what had once been his father's workshop. Around him was only rubble, broken tools, the shattered ribs of an oud. A woman's voice wailed somewhere in a song of despair and grief and mourning. He shut his eyes and tried to remember what it had been like when he'd pillowed his cheek on wood shavings, when his father's friends sat there laughing and drinking tea. Where was his father now, and his mother? They'd been taken away, he knew, but he didn't know where. It was his job to stay in the workshop until they returned, guarding it from further destruction.

It was Rafael who showed him how to smuggle things. Rafael had been one of the leaders of the protests in the first decade of the century and had spent time in jail. He helped Nicolás tape the InScreen to the inside of his upper thigh, right against his scrotum. –Then you go to the bathroom in the jail and remove it and palm it under the grille when the guard isn't looking.

He managed to palm three InScreens that way — one for Kassim and two more for other organizers of the strike. The pictures that came back were terrifying. People beaten, bloodied, unrecognizable, teeth missing, jaws broken. After a while Nicolás couldn't look at them anymore. It was weak, he knew — these were merely images, not the real thing — but he was having nightmares. He took to sleeping with an InScreen taped to his own thigh in case he was arrested.

The demonstrations continued, though his mother — at home now that the schools weren't functioning — begged him not to go. Millions of people up and down the country, and the politicians huddled in their offices not knowing what to do. His sister Núria took over the bread run for several neighbourhoods; his brother Daniel slipped in and out carrying messages that couldn't be entrusted to electronic communications. Nicolás found himself at the meetings of what was left of the Grupo Cinco de Junio: a middle-aged woman called Ana who had once been a nun, and several workers from the furniture factory, and Miriam, a student like himself who was their liaison with the university cells. It was Miriam — tiny, fearless, indefatigable — who came up with the most daring plans. They ought to infiltrate a cabinet meeting, hold the ministers hostage until the prime minister agreed to their demands. Others argued that it would lead, at best, to only token change.

Meanwhile the country was paralyzed. Students had ceased to go to classes, people to work. Most of the police had walked off the job, too, and there was a kind of cheerful anarchy in the streets. People travelled by bicycle or on foot, since there were no longer any oil deliveries. Many shops were boarded up, their owners fled. The Enrejado network was still functioning, though with governments in other countries collapsing the supplies were intermittent.

When Paola's bruised and bloodied face showed up on his InScreen one morning, he knew he had to act. He'd got her involved, after all; she'd taken more risks than he had. He thought first about calling his grandfather — he must have contacts, still, among the upper echelons — but he didn't want to involve an old man, long retired, in this business. Instead he bicycled to the Chamber of Deputies in the middle of the city and asked to speak to his uncle. Fortunately one of the longtime guards there remembered him and allowed him in past the steel barricades and barbed wire.

–Ah, the young revolutionary! His uncle stood up to embrace Nicolás, who pulled away. –Okay. We're enemies. I understand. He lit a cigarette and sat on the edge of his desk.

–No, you don't. You don't understand anything. Nicolás took out his InScreen and showed his uncle the picture of Paola. –How would you feel if that was Caterina?

–Caterina's a sensible girl, we brought her up properly. She isn't mixed up with all this — this holding the country to hostage.

–Paola's brother's a banker, Tío. He probably contributed to your campaign.

His uncle shrugged. –And she broke the law. Which is why she's in jail. He blew smoke, reflectively, at Nicolás. –But I'd feel the same way if I were sleeping with her.

He swung without thinking at his uncle's face, but his uncle caught his wrist with a surprisingly strong grip. –Don't be a fool. Go home, look after your mother. This business is for *niños mimados*, spoiled kids.

Here was another language he didn't know, a language of distortion and stereotype and dismissal. He and his uncle were speaking past each other, on parallel tracks. For a moment he saw his uncle among the thugs who'd destroyed the oud workshop, their faces contorted with fury and disgust and hate.

When he was little — probably on one of those nights when he couldn't sleep — his grandfather had told him a story about a boy who lived in a balloon. He didn't know if his grandfather had made this story up or read it in a book. The boy lived in the balloon with his pet rabbit and floated wherever he wanted. *Where should we go tonight?* his grandfather

would ask, and Nicolás would cry, *Let's go to the mountains!*
And the next minute there they were, hovering above tall
snow-covered peaks where people lived in nests like birds
and served drinks made of crushed ice and moonbeams.

If only he had such a balloon now.

They came for him three nights later. There were four
of them, in balaclavas and civilian clothes, and they pushed
him around and searched the flat while his mother and his
siblings sat huddled in a corner. Then they bundled him
out of the flat and into a waiting van, using their fists on
his face. A bone snapped, loudly, in his cheek; his ears
filled with blood and a strange high-pitched screaming he
recognized, belatedly, as his own. When he came to he was
in a dark cell among others who groaned and muttered and
cried out. He lay there, stunned and battered, until greying
light filled the tiny barred window and the guards came
past, hammering on the doors to wake them up. Opening
his eyes, he looked into the face of one of the members of
the Grupo Cinco de Junio.

–Luis? he said, with what felt like a mouthful of broken
teeth.

Luis helped him sit up and gave him some water and held
him, tenderly. He wanted to weep and couldn't.

How long he spent in the cell he didn't know. Food—
bread and bowls of thin gruel—came at irregular intervals.
New arrivals were brought in, other inmates transferred
out. Somewhere along the way he'd lost his InScreen, so he
couldn't let anyone know where he was. Luis, taken away
on the second day, urged him to remain strong and said
he'd get in touch with Nicolás's family, if he got out. Wild
rumours circulated—that the New Dawn Party had formed
a government and reintroduced capital punishment; that the

prime minister had been assassinated; that the Chamber of Deputies had been torched. Nicolás hoped simultaneously that his family had found out where he was, and that they hadn't. His mother must be worried sick. And Núria...had they come for her, too? He shut out the images of his sister's bleeding face. His whole body ached, the cuts on his face festered and filled with pus. At night he summoned the balloon and floated through the night sky. Below him the cities were spread out like glowing nets thrown over the globe—beautiful nets full of menace, designed to trap small insects like himself.

A new arrival, a grizzled elderly man, brought him a message: *Don't lose heart, help is coming.* The man had no idea who the message was from. Kassim? It seemed unlikely. His family? When nothing happened he decided the message was a mistake. Or perhaps the sender had been arrested, too. Half the city seemed to be incarcerated now, judging from the numbers of new arrestees, the rumours about the mobilization of the army.

One morning the cell door opened and Nicolás was ordered out. Stiff from inactivity, he could hardly walk. The guards took him into a kind of reception area where other guards sat at computer screens, and where a man he didn't recognize stood on the other side of a glass wall. Tall, erect, turning his old Guardia Civil cap in his hands, his face so aged Nicolás could have wept.

—Abuelo, he said, but it came out in an indistinct croak.

The guards led him to a door at the far end of the glass wall and handed him over to his grandfather, who took his arm. —Don't talk, he said, and led Nicolás outside. Around the corner one of the antique motorbikes from the Guardia's early years was parked at the curb. —Here, his grandfather said, and helped him onto the back of the bike. —Can you stay upright? Nicolás put his arms round his grandfather's waist and hung on shakily as they growled their way through the streets, empty except for the soldiers guarding each intersection. At the sight of the old man's cap with its Guardia insignia, they snapped to attention and saluted.

On the outskirts of the city they began a slow climb into the hills. Where were they going? Wherever it was, they were taking back roads rather than the main highways. It was all he could do to hang on and not pass out. The day lengthened; he was starving and dying of thirst; yet still they rode on into a brilliant cold twilight. The stars were coming out when they turned onto a dirt track and entered what must once have been a village, though it stood in ruins. His grandfather pulled up outside one of the derelict houses, parked the bike, and half-carried Nicolás inside. A couple of beds, freshly made up, and a rough table and chairs, and a wood stove. His grandfather helped him to one of the beds and made him lie down. Then he went outside and Nicolás heard the sound of a well handle being pumped. His grandfather came back inside and held a glass of water to Nicolás's parched lips. Afterwards he made a fire in the stove, heated water in a basin, and tenderly bathed Nicolás's battered face.

—*Nieto mío*, he said sorrowfully, over and over. —What have they done to you?

—How did you find out where I was? His voice cracked as though it too had been beaten.

—An old colleague. His grandfather made a dismissive gesture. —We're not all on the side of the government, you know. Those *putas*—yes, I know what you call them... His jaw tightened. –There was respect for the rule of law, once.

He brought Nicolás a bowl of warmed soup, but after a few mouthfuls nausea overwhelmed him; he lay back, exhausted. –Where are we?

–In your great-grandmother's house. Where I grew up. These last weeks I've been restoring it, I thought we might need a refuge.

He had so many other questions—where his mother and Núria and the others were, how his grandfather had got him out—but he must have fallen asleep, because when he woke it was fully dark except for a nearby candle. His grandfather sat there in the flickering light, his hand resting on the quilt. Nicolás couldn't stop his tears.

–Don't waste your energy, *nieto*. You need to regain your strength. You don't suppose we're just going to roll over and let them win, do you?

–You're turning into a revolutionary, Nicolás murmured, smiling. –You, of all people!

–Christ was a revolutionary too, wasn't he? He was on the side of the ruled, not the rulers. Listen, I brought you something, I know how much it means to you.

From a corner his grandfather brought out an old leather case decorated in Arabic letters. Nicolás didn't have the strength to open it, so his grandfather did it for him. He lay with his arms round the instrument, watching the shadows on the walls. His grandfather, sitting by his bed, began singing some ancient song, one Nicolás thought he remembered from childhood, something about exile and lost love. He didn't try to puzzle out the old words. Instead he burrowed deeper under the blankets and held the cracked oud close. Under his grandfather's voice, if he listened hard, he could make out another, just barely audible — his father's in his workshop, speaking that strange language, the two voices weaving in and out until he was no longer sure which was which.

SIGNS
AND
PORTENTS

SPEAKING IN TONGUES

She was carrying the mail up the path to the house when she noticed. It was imprinted on the inside of her wrist, like the pale echo of a bar code. She must have been clutching some flyer or other too tightly, and it had transferred to her skin. At the kitchen counter Boas danced round her as she sorted, demanding his walk. Fall mornings, on the island, meant flocks of sandpipers and rain dripping from the arbutus trees, not the ancient chestnuts under the limestone clock tower, the murmurations of students. She took down the leash, eliciting excited barks, and stepped outside again. She'd been retired for eight years — had been pushed out, none too gently, at seventy-five — but September still brought a quickening excitement, a sharpening of the mind. The sharpening had begun with her father, a classical scholar who taught her the rudiments of Latin before she could read English, and in his honour she enlivened a dozen new pencils every Labour Day.

In the afternoons, staving off senility, she sat at her desk with the sharpened pencils and worked on a long-delayed paper, "Lenition in Kwak'wala and Anishinaabemowin." Her mother had drifted into early dementia, though her father had done crosswords until he was ninety-two—had left one uncompleted the morning of his death, which no doubt infuriated him. The desk faced west over the Georgia Strait in the cabin built to his specifications, a large window let into each octagonal wall, the San Juan Islands a blue haze beyond. As a child she'd spun herself dizzy on her father's office chair above that view. These days Torin did the same thing, his feet tucked up, giggling.

Somehow, without noticing, she'd reached the beach. A yacht floated across her line of vision. Boas, with a Scottish terrier's disapproval of water, made little growling forays into the waves, carrying the stick she'd thrown. There was the ferry, bleating its regular crossing from the mainland. She ploughed along the sand, head down, looking for sea glass. A large jar of it sat on her windowsill, added to mostly on Torin's visits. There—what was that bit of yellow? Too opaque to be glass. Still, she lifted it from its indentation, rubbed it clean with her thumb. The perfect whorl of a snail shell that shouldn't be here—*Littorina obtusata*, the northern yellow periwinkle. Shouldn't be, but was.

An uncle, a marine biologist, had brought her to this beach at night with a flashlight. He'd lifted the checkered periwinkle, *Littorina scutulata*, from the tide pools to show her the tiny rake for gathering algae that pulsed in and out of its mouth. But this one, *Littorina obtusata*, was an Atlantic coast species, introduced from Britain in the ballast of nineteenth-century ships. What was it doing here?

At the house she washed off the shell and checked her copy of Harbo's *Shells and Shellfish of the Pacific Northwest*. No mention of northern yellow periwinkles migrating, somehow, to the west coast. But unexpected things turned up on the beach all the time. Once, inexplicably, the carcass of an Asian house shrew, identified by a zoologist from a mainland university. There was bound to be some sort of explanation.

The paper — the staver-off of decrepitude — was supposed to be delivered in Berlin, in November, at an international congress on comparative linguistics. Which meant suitcases, hotels, flying at thirty thousand feet above the earth — the tired apparatus of the physical body, dragged through a particularly modern hell. Did she really want to spend the time she had left in airtight conference rooms, enduring a disrupted digestive system? She wanted to master the tasks she'd set herself in old age: throwing pots on a wheel, raising plants in a greenhouse. Tasks for her hands and eyes, those concrete organs that she'd always taken for granted and might now be taken away at any minute.

At five p.m. she lifted herself out of the maze of linguistic symbols and made tea. And then it was evening — time to heat up soup, to take a last walk with Boas before bed, to study the stars. At night, outside, she imagined star languages in their billions, their sound waves travelling through the cosmos. She kept up, as much as she could, with quantum physics, knew about the many-worlds theory and was certain that, after her death, universes would unfold from one another like origami, suddenly visible in earthly dimensions. What a fascinating job that would be — first interpreter to some distant star-circling planet!

The stars, tonight, were hidden by cloud. She studied the dark shapes of the trees instead, the rough wood fence that separated her property from her neighbour's. For a moment, in the sideways V of a branch, she saw the fifth letter of the Arabic alphabet as written at the beginning of a word. A hanging leaf provided the dot underneath.

Too long in her head again. She was seeing symbols in everything.

That evening, washing herself before bed, she discovered the imprint, unfaded, still there on her wrist. No amount of soap would remove it.

In the morning, showering, she noticed the second. Not like a bar code, this time, but a series of greyish squiggles on the back of her left knee. She'd never have seen it if she hadn't bent sideways to retrieve the soap. Examined in a mirror, it resembled a cursive script in an alphabet she didn't recognize. It, too, resisted repeated scrubbing. Perhaps it was an allergic reaction. Or was there some disease that manifested as grey letters on the skin?

She could ask her doctor, but that meant the tedium of appointments and explanations and tests. A nuisance, when she had so little time. *Go away*, she told the marks. *Stop being a bother. Don't make demands.*

With Torin's help she was learning how to write simple computer code, another hedge against senescence. He was her son Gregor's oldest child, dispatched to the west coast at every opportunity since his mother's death, six years before, from a rare heart defect. Some days, staring at the strings of symbols, she wondered, despairingly, if a binary language was the future. Some days her brain shut down and refused to respond at all. An hour of computer coding was always followed by an hour's walk with Boas, ending in town at the bakery, where Torin got to choose a treat and she got to watch him eat it.

In early October she picked him up at the airport in Vancouver. The rain so drenching it seemed a monsoon, the windshield liquefying on the drive back to the ferry. Unperturbed, Torin told her about learning to play the trumpet, the aquarium they'd set up at home, his new friend Firdaus, who came from Iran. As usual they didn't speak of his stepmother, or of the new half-sister, now almost two.

They were eating dinner in the ferry café when he noticed the mark on her wrist.

–That's so cool, Babs, he told her, and rolled up his sleeve. (Babs, always — Barbara was for her academic papers — because she refused to be Grandma or Nanny or Gran.) The inside of his elbow bore a similar string of symbols, darker and less complex than her own. –Firdaus has one too, he said matter-of-factly. –Inside his mouth.

–His mouth? she heard herself say weakly.

–*I* think they're messages. Torin reached for another of the little paper tubs of ketchup. –About saving the world. He looked sombrely at his grandmother. –Everyone knows the planet's dying.

Was *this* what eleven-year-olds talked about these days between their texting and their computer games? Perhaps the use of binary code was altering the brain. Perhaps each day's news was driving them crazy with anxiety.

–Eat your broccoli, she said firmly, as if the rules of the old world still applied. They didn't, of course. She just didn't know what the new ones were.

Ø

Caught up in explorations of soggy trails, in Thanksgiving dinner with friends and children and assorted others, they didn't speak about it again until the third day of Torin's visit. She'd been debating whether to show him the mark behind her knee, but when she did he was unsurprised.

–Of course you get more of them. You're older. And you know all those languages. They've probably decided you'll figure them out eventually.

–Who, she said, not sure she wanted to ask, are *they*?

–Firdaus thinks they're from another galaxy. Trying to help us out. Torin was scrolling through messages on his cellphone. –And Olivia thinks they're whales.

–*Whales*? She felt as if she were falling into a crevasse in some peculiar landscape, so deep she'd never be able to climb out. Perhaps another dimension was opening up after all, and this was how it felt?

–Olivia has one under her arm. Torin lifted his own arm, pointing at a place near the armpit. –Just a short one, though. She got it one night, it woke her up. It was itching.

Babs had read about cases of mass hysteria, groups of people spontaneously manifesting the same physical symptoms — vomiting, for example, or dizziness, or seizures. There'd been those dancing plagues in the Middle Ages, in Germany and Switzerland and France, when people danced uncontrollably for days or weeks. During the first Gulf War there'd been episodes of nausea and fainting in several elementary schools in the States. Was that what this was — contagious psychogenic illness? But Torin's last visit had been in July, and the marks on her wrist hadn't appeared till fall.

–Olivia, she found herself saying, has a very vivid imagination. That disapproving tone — she hadn't meant to sound like that at all. –Have you told your parents?

–Of course not. Her stupidity had offended him; he was frowning. –They wouldn't believe us. They're the wrong age, anyway.

–For what?

–For getting the messages.

It was a neighbour's daughter who found the second periwinkle. Torin had gone home the day before, and she'd dropped round at Francine's to pick up her weekly egg supply. (Francine kept free-range Buff Orpingtons.)

–Look what Deirdre found, at Roxmere Point, Francine said, and held out a tiny whorled shell, yellow and orange. –Odd, isn't it? I've never seen these here before.

It was a deeper shade this time, with its characteristic flattened spire, the shell curling round itself. Someone must have dumped them on the beaches as a practical joke. Or to get rid of some old collection.

–Yes, I found one, too, on the beach near my place, she said casually. –They must have washed up from somewhere.

Deirdre found a third periwinkle and then a fourth, and brought them over to show Babs. At twelve she was turning leggy and exuberant, with hair the pale creamy colour of the fourth shell. Babs told her about the nineteenth-century sailing ships, and how they must be from someone's eastern collection. –I'm writing down where I found them, and in what position, Deirdre said. –They mean something. I don't know what yet, but they do.

–That's preposterous, she said sharply, regretting it the minute Deirdre flinched. –What I mean is...What *did* she mean? –You can find meaning in anything if you want to.

–But you know lots of different languages, Deirdre said quietly. –And they all have meaning, don't they?

–Yes, but... She was floundering, back in that crevasse. –They're *languages*. These are just—shells.

The Tlingit had a word, *yalooleit*, that meant coffin or womb as well as bivalve shell. The Haida believed that the first men sprang from a cockle shell when the trickster, Raven, opened it. The Navajo held that Changing Woman, the source of life and fertility, was washed ashore and emerged from a seashell. Perhaps the old gods were stirring, unable to sleep. Tilting the world so that shells turned up in unexplained places, creating confusion everywhere, a kind of cosmic joke.

Though that didn't explain the skin symbols. Perhaps that, too, was one of Raven's tricks.

On his next visit—it was spring break—Torin didn't speak about the messages. In the unseasonably warm March weather they skipped stones across the bay, ate battered halibut at the diner, and had Torin's friends over to play an old-fashioned game of Monopoly (at her insistence; it would limit their exposure to the screen). Afterwards, expertly manipulating strands of pizza cheese, they talked, knowledgeably, about sea monsters, pet lizards, how birds had evolved from dinosaurs.

Deirdre and Torin were sitting on the beach the next morning, heads together, whispering, oblivious, when she arrived with Boas. Torin was never up this early—he always slept in. She approached uneasily, pretending to be absorbed in Boas's fetch game.

–It's only Babs, Torin said.

Deirdre held out a palm. –Another shell, look! Torin found this one.

It was large and lemon-yellow, a golden sea jewel. –We were trying to figure out, me and Deirdre, how many languages there are, Torin explained. –I mean, there's the skin codes and the shells, and there must be others.

An uncontrollable shiver seized her, a vertiginous terror about what these children were up to. She squatted down beside them. Boas shoved his nose between legs, eager not to be left out. –What, she said, is going on? Is this some sort of—I don't know, some stunt?

Torin looked genuinely puzzled. –I told you. They're messages.

Beside him Deirdre, staring at the shell in her palm, nodded slowly.

–But how do you know that? I mean, what evidence do you have? She couldn't help it, that training of hers, the primacy of empirical fact. It was what she knew how to do.

–We just... Torin and Deirdre glanced at each other. Torin shrugged, and Deirdre looked away. –We just *know*, that's all, Torin said.

It was some credulous cult, on a par with religious fundamentalism or right-wing ideologies. A nationwide childish conspiracy. She stood up. You couldn't reason with such beliefs. –Boas is getting restless, she said, which wasn't true. –I'd better keep going. What would you like for breakfast, Torin?

That evening, taking off her bra, she discovered a third outbreak of the skin symbols, a ragged line that looked almost like a sentence and travelled right round her left breast.

Perhaps it was some unexplained dermopathy, Miranda said in her melting-butter voice. Babs was grateful for the lack of judgement in this generation of doctors. A variant of Morgellons disease, possibly, though that was believed to be a delusional parasitosis.

—But certain metals can produce this effect too, Miranda said. The flowered headband that held back her spiralling hair made her look even younger. —Do you wear gold regularly?

On some people, apparently, friction with gold alloys could result in what looked like black lines. But the only gold Babs had worn for the last fifty-two years was her wedding ring, without problems.

—It's definitely odd. Miranda wrote something on her doctor's pad. —You don't seem like a candidate for hysteria. I'm going to refer you to a specialist.

At home Babs wrote down all the symbols as clearly as she could, using a mirror where she had to and then reversing them. She would treat this like a linguist, as though it *were* a language. Defeat the children at their own game. Establish that it was, after all, some nonsense eruption, some peculiar virus that mimicked meaning. The marks weren't all equally readable, though she was quite sure they hadn't faded. Some resembled Cyrillic and Hebrew characters, but others she couldn't identify at all—bars and circles and what looked like tiny ideograms. A hodgepodge, with no rhyme or reason she could see.

She phoned a former colleague, someone she thought she could trust, and sent him the transcription. He couldn't make any sense of it, either.

—I suspect it's some sort of allergy or pathogen that mimics writing, Babs. His voice held a faint tinge of alarm, or was that her imagination? —It doesn't look like any sort of coherent system. I mean, ideograms *and* an alphabet?

The next morning she found a periwinkle shell — was this the fifth? — on her doorstep. Boas tasted it and promptly spat it out. She carried it inside and laid it next to the first one on her windowsill. That evening she searched for the spirals of shells among the glyphs she'd transcribed from her skin, but found none.

There were many writings that couldn't be deciphered, of course. The Vinča script, for example, found on artifacts excavated near the Yugoslavian city. It was thought to be between 6,500 and 8,000 years old, but no one knew what the language was. Or the Harappa script, which had been used in the valley of the Indus River between 3500 and 2000 BC, though whether the symbols represented a language or something else was unknown. There was even a script that might be a practical joke. The Voynich Manuscript, according to different researchers, was the record of early discoveries by the thirteenth-century friar Roger Bacon, written in a peculiarly complicated code; a rare prayer book from the Cathars, written in a pidgin version of a Germanic/Romance creole; or meaningless strings of characters, a joke played on the Holy Roman Emperor Rudolf II of Habsburg, who had supposedly acquired the manuscript for six hundred ducats.

Ø

Torin, she remembered, had a book about code-breaking given to him on his last birthday. When she asked him, though, he looked at her with amused condescension. –You think that's what we're doing? Inventing codes?

They were sitting together on a bench overlooking the ocean after one of Boas's outings. She pleated and unpleated Boas's leash. –I thought it was a possibility.

Though that didn't, of course, explain the eruptions on her own body. Fortunately Torin didn't point out the contradiction.

–Why is Boas named Boas? He was bored, slouching, almost adolescent; she didn't have much time left to have real conversations with him. –Dad says he's named after a linguist.

–Franz Boas. A remarkable man. A nineteenth-century German Jew who studied the Kwakwaka'wakw language here on the coast, and believed you could only formulate theories and conclusions *after* rigorous examination of the evidence. You haven't answered my question.

–We told you already. His body tightened, a shield against discovery. –You haven't said anything to Dad, have you?

–No, of course not. She made a face at him. –But you must admit it's all a bit—a bit—

–*I* think it's amazing. His eyes glowed like a fanatic's. –That we're getting help.

Boas was nose-greeting an acquaintance, a ringleted English sheepdog who lowered a noble head. Babs had argued with friends over the use of *who* or *that* in talking about Boas. –They're beings, she'd said hotly. –Animals, just as we are. *That* is for things. Boas is most certainly not a thing.

—But it's not much help if you can't read these—these messages, is it?

Torin was staring out to sea, his eyes narrowed. —Deirdre says I ought to ask *you*. I mean, you're getting them too, not just kids.

—As a matter of fact... She described her colleague's response, her doctor's.

He gave a theatrical sigh. —It's something completely new, Babs. *They* don't know. How could they?

It was starting to rain. The owner of the sheepdog flicked up her hood and waved goodbye. Boas nudged Babs' leg with his nose in his own language, one she'd learned slowly and stupidly.

—Can we go to Martina's? Torin was hungry again despite the thick soup and four slices of bread she'd fed him at lunch. At Martina's they made fat vegetarian burgers slathered with their own special mayonnaise.

She stood up slowly, her joints squeaking in their own code. —Only, she said, if you tell me all about these marks on your friends.

Francine was standing on a ladder painting a wall of her kitchen when Babs dropped by. She'd left Torin at the airport security gate the day before, none the wiser, though he'd given her detailed descriptions of the marks.

—Deirdre's found nine of those shells, did you know? Francine said, pouring coffee into a paint-smeared mug. —Counting your two, that is. She keeps rearranging them. Trying to figure out what they say.

Babs sipped her coffee cautiously. —Don't you think it's a little—peculiar?

–Obsessive, yes. But that's their age, don't you think?

Apparently Deirdre had told her mother she wouldn't find any more periwinkles; there would only be nine. The number nine, according to a cousin of Francine's ex—an astrobiologist at Yale—represented the ability to see clearly and the integration of the three worlds: physical, intellectual, spiritual. It was also the last symbol before the return to unity, represented by zero.

–Deirdre says that's the job of this generation. Making the planet whole again. I'm impressed, I must say. Sounds like a major task to me.

Francine had also consulted professionals—the school counsellor, in her case. Children had changed alarmingly over the last decade or so, he told her; his colleagues had noticed too. How quick they were to grow up, how fascinated by interspecies communication and other worlds. How they had skills like telepathy and precognition.

–And the weirdest thing, Francine said. –I've noticed this with Deirdre and her friend Stella: they can make a streetlamp go out when they walk by. She got up to feed the cat as if they were merely talking about the weather and not a shift on the world's axis. –Especially the amber sodium vapour type. Because of the make-up of their body's bioelectromagnetic field, so I'm told.

It was a great relief to Babs, on Torin's next visit, that no streetlights faltered when they took Boas for his evening walk.

Fresh air, she decided. Fresh air and excursions and physical exercise. When Torin came for his summer holidays they'd get outside as much as possible. For his twelfth birthday in

June she sent him a subscription to *Scientific American* and a lavishly illustrated book called *Our Physical World*. She would hold him down with her on solid earth as long as possible. Geoffrey, his late grandfather, dead these twenty years—an unfashionably non-hyphenated geologist—had exhibited the same disconnectedness, the same dreamy absences. Torin had also inherited his grandfather's thin pinched nose, though his sharply angled jaw came from his mother. His half-mocking, half-confiding look was hers too, as though at some shared and absurd conviction.

But Torin did not come that summer after all, because Babs got sick. It began with dizziness, and a ringing in her ears, and a strange taste in her throat like very salty seaweed. Miranda referred her to a neurotologist, who suspected Ménière's disease. The dizziness, and the strange taste, got worse. A half-dozen tests proved inconclusive. The neurotologist prescribed betahistine and referred her to a colleague of his in West Vancouver. A highly puzzling constellation of symptoms, the colleague said. She hadn't come across anything similar in the literature.

The betahistine helped but made her nauseous and brought out a blistery rash behind her ears that wouldn't go away. The three skin marks—there were, after all, only three—remained, though no one seemed interested or thought they had anything to do with her illness. Francine and her other friends, emissaries from the land of health, brought her meals, did her laundry, kept her company. Even Deirdre, now thirteen, came and read aloud to her in the evenings. Deirdre had acquired a boyfriend, though according to her mother they seemed quite uninterested in sex. They researched things online—planetary exploration, the origin of stars, the composition of sand. Why weren't they practising French kissing instead, Francine wanted to know?

Deirdre was going through a stage of dystopian fantasy novels, grim worlds where children were tortured or imprisoned or pursued by an increasingly inventive panoply of monsters, but nevertheless survived. *They're rehearsing, these children*, Babs thought, and then reminded herself how she too had loved death and mystery and darkness at that age, a backdrop for her own blazing self.

A week later the specialist in West Vancouver sent her an email. *A very interesting article in the literature recently. Children in several Midwest American cities reporting symptoms like yours. Some of them have peculiar cravings—for dirt or soil, for example. The authors hypothesize either a mineral deficiency or some new autoimmune pathology.*

The specialist had included a link to the article. Babs, half-lying against her sofa cushions, clicked on it. The jargon was almost impenetrable, nearly as bad as her own profession's, and she fell asleep with the glow of the laptop flooding her, as if she faced an altar.

Deirdre arrived as usual that evening, bringing a basket of fresh peaches and her collection of shells. Babs had almost forgotten about them. As it turned out, so had Deirdre, who'd given up on the idea of messages and was instead learning how to repair bicycles with her new boyfriend.

—How is he, your boyfriend? Babs asked, struggling to sit upright on the sofa. Bryn or Bryant or some such—she could never remember this generation's unorthodox names.

—Bevan, said Deirdre. —Bevan Eiric Alinsky. He's fine,

thanks. He's spending a couple of weeks with his grandparents in Winnipeg.

It was stinkingly hot, with unusually high humidity. Peculiar weather for the island; climate change, of course. —Should I turn the light on? Deirdre asked.

—No, it's cooler like this, in the dark. She'd had the shades drawn all day, the fan whirring beside her; the cabin had no air conditioning. Who had ever thought, here, it might be needed?

—I brought you these to show you, Deirdre said, opening the paper bag she held and tipping the contents into Babs' hand. She felt rather than saw the cool smoothness of the shells, their sharp little rims. —It's hard to see in this light, Deirdre said, but they've changed colour.

Babs examined them in the beam of Deirdre's pen flashlight. They had darkened, each of them, to rich browns and ochres that were almost black. —Is this what they do over time, do you think? Deirdre asked. —Once you take them from the beach?

They checked the shells against the two on Babs' windowsill. These had darkened too, though not as much. —I looked online, Deirdre said, but I couldn't find anything. She frowned, puzzling, touching them gently. —They must be telling us something again. I wish we could understand.

The old knowledge, the stuff that had carried them from the Enlightenment, was drying out and blowing away. In its stead was a new kind of knowledge, thrusting itself in their faces, demanding to be deciphered and understood. What was needed now were seers, diviners, poets; the trouble was, Babs didn't know any. She knew people like herself, who had parsed knowledge by dividing it into ever smaller pieces and had no idea, now, how to put it all back together.

Ø

A certain Dr. Molly Threshwick at her old university was a folklorist with an international reputation. Babs knew her from interdepartmental committees. She found herself telling Molly Threshwick, by email, about the discovery of an Atlantic periwinkle species on a Pacific coast, and about Deirdre and her grandson, though she left out the part about the marks on her own body. After she'd hit *send* she had immediate regrets. She was a fool after all, a credulous old woman, evincing, despite her efforts, mental deterioration and decline.

A week passed, ten days. When the reply came, she couldn't at first bring herself to open it. Molly Threshwick, it turned out, had been away at a conference on new developments in the study of proto-writing systems, of all things. Babs would be aware, she said, of archetypal beliefs about marine shells, apparently universal, such as their association with birth images. Human embryos, like snails in the ocean, dwelt in the salty environment of amniotic fluid. Representations of gods or humans emerging from shells were widespread in ancient Mesoamerica as well as Peru, India, and possibly other places. In the Sacred Well at Chichén Itzá was a gold plaque showing an old man emerging from a snail shell, suggesting the arrival in the world of hidden knowledge.

Did she know, Dr. Threshwick asked at the end of her email, what Erasmus Darwin — grandfather of the more famous Charles — had written? *E conchis omnia*. Everything from shells.

The taste of seaweed lingered, but Babs got no worse. By September, when her energy had returned enough to take Boas for short walks, she asked if Torin might miss a week of school and come to stay with her. He arrived bearing gifts that must have been chosen by his stepmother—herbal tea from a specialty store, a lavender-infused pillow, a new book about Turkey, which she'd always wanted to visit. He was cheerful and insouciant. She listened to everything he said with great care and said little. On their first evening they went to Martina's and took Deirdre with them. Talked about island news—Deirdre was hand-rearing an orphaned lamb, she and Bevan were just friends now—while Torin asked eager questions. Over dessert—Martina's famous rhubarb crumble—Babs asked, tentatively, if any more of the marks had appeared on Torin's friends.

–They're all fading, Torin said without interest.

–*I* think you just didn't figure them out in time, Deirdre said firmly. –It's all so new. They'll try something else instead.

–What about the shells? Babs asked before she could stop herself.

Deirdre stirred her mound of ice cream into the rhubarb. –They're changing again. She paused, as if she wasn't sure whether to continue. –They're glowing. I take them out at night to watch.

–Hey, cool! said Torin enthusiastically. –Can I come over later and see them?

–They send out pulses. She stared at her spoon as if it was glowing too. –On and off. And then they stop.

Babs had no doubt that the gods her generation had worshipped were dying. They were passing away, were emptying out into husks. The new ones, when the time came, would stride out onto land, perhaps on this very island, full of vigour, shining in their nakedness. She wondered if she'd live long enough to see it. They were readying themselves, the children, they were paying attention. They were doing what they had to do. They looked back at her from wherever they were, their faces radiant, but they couldn't tell her where it was.

BRING DOWN
YOUR ANGELS
AND SET ME FREE

The man appeared on her lawn on a Wednesday in October. He emerged from the mist moving in from the lake, the shifting light, a bent figure with a pickaxe. Thirty-something probably, muscled arms in shirt sleeves, flat grey cap above a small square jaw. Charlotte went outside and walked through the tatters of mist toward him, or toward where she'd seen him, but he'd gone. Baffled, mildly irritated, she returned to the house. She was shivering in her T-shirt; the day had turned raw.

The next time, a week or so later, she was backing out of the driveway, late for an appointment. He stood holding his pickaxe in the corner by the Japanese maple. Turned and looked at her as she drove past. What she noticed now were the thin ribs, the eyes narrowed, hunted. The eyes gave her pause. She phoned the city works department. No, they had no one working on William Street. That evening, over a dinner meeting, one of her colleagues said –A *pickaxe*? What would he be doing with a pickaxe nowadays?

Charlotte could have imagined the pickaxe but not the man. He reminded her of her brother, her tall intense younger brother, a sculptor in Halifax. She was overtired, it was true; her last mission, to the Gambia, had taken a lot out of her. Her colleague said —I wish they'd take a pickaxe to *my* street! One pothole after another since the winter we had.

The house was a two-storey limestone saltbox with a glossy red door and black-and-white trim, the ivy thick on the walls, and had once belonged to a British officer who'd fought in the War of 1812. Charlotte had grown up with the insubstantiality of wood; the house, built in 1815, looked as though it could withstand anything. The owner had inherited it from his great-aunt and wanted a quick sale. That red door, and the ivy—she'd bought it on impulse the day she'd seen it. Her share of the sale of her parents' house on the west coast would more than cover the down payment.

—That British officer probably helped dispatch some of my ancestors, she told Campbell when he came for a visit a week after the sale went through.

—Don't blame me when you start having nightmares. He lifted his scotch glass, the first of the night, to her. —Channelling your forebears and all that. Around them the bar hummed angrily, an agitated hive.

—My nightmares, she said, are about totally other things. Like yours. When are you off to South Sudan? She didn't tease, this time, about him being a war whore—his term — though it was true. He'd been a stringer for Agence France-Presse when they'd met in Cameroon; she'd been part of a UN child malnutrition campaign.

–Next week. My editor thinks it's a waste of time, no one's interested in another failed-state story. Even if the details keep changing.

–There's an orphanage in Yei run by a group of French nuns, she said. Campbell was already signalling the bartender; she put her fingers over her own glass. –Amazing place, my friend Jeannette was with a team there a while back. You could do a story about them.

–Another of your Charlottes living there? Campbell's old conceit, that there were babies named after her all over Africa.

She laughed. –I've never worked in South Sudan. There might be the odd Jeannette, though. Who knows, if you write a good piece they might name one after you, too.

–Poor little sod. The Campbells were a ruthless bunch. He might not be pleased when he finds out.

Who'd have thought, with her peripatetic life, that she'd ever own a house? She'd spent the last dozen years nursing in Chad, Guinea-Bissau, Botswana—countries most people she knew had barely heard of and certainly couldn't have found on a map. When she went back to Canada she stood paralyzed in grocery aisles among fluorescent-green broccoli, waxen apples, unable to have a normal conversation. No Canadian doctor would understand the numbness, the anger, the inability to sleep. What did you talk about when you'd spent three months in acute hospitalization tents, setting up IV drips with rehydration salts for one cholera patient after another? When you'd seen a pregnant young mother—feverish, malnourished—who'd trekked fifty miles through rebel-held territory to give birth? Or helped treat a badly dehydrated three-year-old, her arm suppurating through to the bone from Buruli ulcer?

It was Buruli ulcer — of all things — that had brought her to this city in the first place. A Nigerian colleague from her early days in the field was presenting his research on *Mycobacterium ulcerans* at the medical school. She'd driven him down from Toronto, and afterwards they'd walked along the lakeshore together. It was Emmanuel's first visit to Canada, but when she saw the house with its *For Sale* sign he understood. He even wrote out a prescription, laughing, saying she'd have to frame it because no one would be able to fill it.

–The house is what I prescribe for you, he said. –The house will be your medicine. Though a person must want to be healed. The mind and the body must collaborate, no?

–And the soul, she said. –Don't forget the soul.

–The house, he said, the house will nourish that. The house will provide.

She kept being sent on missions and the house stood empty, her boxes still unpacked. When she next took a break it was August, stifling, humid. She'd come from a week's holiday with friends in South Africa, where the winter weather was cool and invigorating. Between boxes she sat drinking margaritas in the back garden, now overrun with daisies and delphiniums and unpruned raspberry canes. What had she been thinking, buying a house in this eastern city on the shores of a vast lake where the streets were named after dead British generals and forgotten royalty? Her own ancestors were refugees from potato famines and land clearances, not men and women who'd fled north from a revolution to a country where they could still be loyal to the Crown. Besides, with its four bedrooms, its vast dining room, its walk-in pantry, it was far too big for her. But there was nothing to send her back to the west coast—her parents dead, her sister in Australia, her sculptor brother busy carving out his own life along with his works of granite.

What she needed was a roommate, someone to animate the place while she was away. Was that what Emmanuel had meant with his prescription? And a dog—she'd wanted a dog since childhood. With all her travelling it hadn't seemed sensible, but if the roommate liked dogs . . . She'd get a stray from the shelter. Name him Crofton, after the British officer.

When the doorbell rang the next morning, for a strange unstrung moment she saw the man on her lawn. What did *he* want? But a tall young woman stood there, a good six inches taller than Charlotte, lifting a rope of dark hair from her cheek. –I saw your sign. Is the room still available?

–The sign? Charlotte stared at her, unmoored by the young woman's poise, her obvious solidity.

–I rang the bell last week but there was no one here. And now the sign's gone. I'm Bethany, by the way.

The house itself must have drawn her, just as Emmanuel had predicted it would. Bethany turned out, happily, to be a third-year economics student, too practical to be given to visions of men on lawns. Her father, she told Charlotte over tea, was a partner at an investment brokerage in Toronto. –Monnier Dettweil, perhaps you've heard of it? I'll be joining him when I graduate. She laughed, a generous unstudied laugh. –Monnier, very funny, huh? Everyone says we must have made it up. It's French, of course.

Had Bethany Monnier's ancestors raised their muskets against the British, perhaps on these very shores? Now she and Charlotte sat drinking tea as Bethany explained her need for quieter roommates. –You'll want a deposit. She laid half an inch of crisp bills on the kitchen table. Taking charge, having determined that Charlotte did not know the ropes. –Will that be enough?

She hadn't even seen the room, but the house was perfect. She'd known the minute she saw it.

–Do you like dogs? Charlotte said.

She joined a new team in the DRC, in North Kivu, coping with the ever-present malaria, an epidemic of measles, a steady influx of rape victims. After her shifts she lay awake in the staff tent, smoking the cigarettes she had promised herself she'd give up. Not twenty miles away were boys of eleven and twelve, armed with AK-47s and M16s and rocket-propelled grenades, part of a rebel force high on amphetamines, on cane juice and gunpowder. Any day now the team would be ordered out for their own safety.

Was it perverse that she liked having her brain numbed, razed as if by some scorched-earth tactic? That she felt more alive here? In a matter of hours she could be in that cool limestone house on the shores of a peaceful lake where, in oblivious ease, she might drink tea with Bethany, pull weeds in her garden. Soldiers in Canadian army uniforms walked unarmed in the streets there, among the shoppers and traffic, ordinary men and women protecting other Canadians from the knowledge she and Campbell had acquired. A knowledge that *war*, that tiny word with its three letters, didn't quite accommodate.

Or perhaps war had always been some variant of this ecstatic embrace of death, this worship of erasure? *I am become Death, the destroyer of worlds.*

One of the local health workers went back to her village to check on her family. When Nadège returned, face drawn, eyes glazed, Charlotte brought her a rice beer and rubbed her back while she sobbed.

—They come up to me, they are holding their guns like big men. Nadège spat out the words in little bursts, as if their flavour sickened her. —And they are singing, singing about victory.

She'd found nothing but piles of smoking embers, blackened bodies in the streets. Her sister's family had fled. She didn't know where her parents were. She'd treated two of the rebels, stragglers from the larger force, for shrapnel wounds, and so they spared her.

Charlotte hadn't been back from the DRC a week when she saw the man on her lawn again. Still with his pickaxe, his hunted eyes, though this time he stood among the fallen pods of a sycamore in the disorder of the back garden. She closed the curtain, afraid he'd turn and look directly at her with that expression of his. Went on with her stripping of the wallpaper in the upstairs bathroom where the plumber had been dismantling the old iron pipes.

Under the wallpaper, yellowed against the lath, was part of a page torn from some long-ago newspaper, layout cramped, print tiny. Halfway down was a headline: *Staff of Streatfeild House Join the Gallant War Effort. This* house, her house, evidently, with its name — now disappeared — engraved on the lintel, just visible above the men ranged on the steps in the photo. A head gardener from a different age gazed out at her, along with two assistant gardeners, a chauffeur, a garden boy, who looked no older than fourteen. Under the cap of the boy she saw the immature face of the man on her lawn, a younger, sweeter face with an air of solemnity, perhaps at the gravity of having his photograph taken.

His name was Thomas Evans. He and his older brother Eddie—one of the assistant gardeners—were enlisting with the Twenty-First Battalion, Canadian Expeditionary Forces. Two boys of eighteen and nineteen from a farm family of nine, exchanging their hoes and pruning shears for rifles and puttees and the honour of serving the King in the Empire's quarrel with the Hun.

Perhaps the soldiering explained the hunted eyes, though not the pickaxe.

But why had he chosen her?

Crofton—the dog, not the British officer—arrived a week after Bethany did. Charlotte and Bethany picked him out together. He was some sort of terrier mix, with magnificent eyebrows and an air of being unfazed by anything.

−Very undignified, said Bethany, looking at the name on the cage, which was Popcorn. −I think he'll be happy to be Crofton.

He took immediately to his new home, digging holes beneath the carefully transplanted azalea bush and commandeering the overstuffed armchair by the window. Joined Charlotte's runs on rural roads and wooded trails, tearing through the undergrowth and attacking defenceless branches. Bethany, in the overgrown garden, taught him to fetch and sit, to come when called. They played chase games through the leggy daisies. Afterwards Bethany sprawled full-length in the grass as Crofton—Croftie, now—crept under the raspberry canes to eat berries, looking round guiltily as if he couldn't believe he wouldn't be stopped.

The original Crofton—Lieutenant-Colonel James Baskermayne Crofton—would not have been amused. He came from a landed family in Cheshire and had joined the Forty-Ninth Regiment of Foot in 1797 by way of purchase of a commission. Sent to Upper Canada, he was appointed aide-de-camp to General Brock himself, receiving a mention in dispatches after the Battle of Queenston Heights. The handsome limestone house had been built for him on land he'd been granted in what was then a village of a thousand people. But within the year he'd been recalled to England, where in 1860 he died in his bed on his Cheshire estate, aged eighty-three.

—We have to buy flowers, Anneke said. —Here, it's where I always get them.

They were standing, Anneke and Charlotte, next to a stall beside a canal, the overcast skies greying the water. Anneke spoke in Dutch to the owner, wrapped in a heavy coat against the damp, and the three of them chose frilled pink-and-white tulips, yellow irises, chrysanthemums in rust-edged porcelain blue.

—Every time I come home I fill the flat with them. Anneke bent her face to the blossoms. —To get rid of the smell of chlorine.

—And does it work?

—It's in your nose, isn't it. Anneke's smile dimmed for a moment. —It never goes away. But I pretend.

Charlotte, who found the smell of chlorine and bleach comforting, studied the tulips. Anneke was right; the flowers were a solace, however temporary. —You need to visit, she'd told Charlotte by email, exercising her clinician's prerogative. And Charlotte, obedient not to a trauma psychologist but to friendship, flew to Amsterdam on her way home from the DRC.

On the way back to the flat they bought ingredients for dinner: fresh chard, an aged gouda cheese, spicy Surinamese piccalilli. Anneke's daughter, studying fashion and design at AMFI, was joining them after classes.

—My other ritual is visiting the Vermeers at the Rijksmuseum. They make me sane again. At least—Anneke's wonderful giggle filled the corner shop—*I* think so, but maybe you'd better ask Liesbeth.

Liesbeth, chopping tomatoes in the impeccable kitchen, turned out to have a variant of her mother's face, with its wide forehead and flared nostrils, and—so Anneke said—her father's blond curls, cropped short. Of course she'd chosen a field unlike her mother's; she had no desire to be a martyr. She glanced slyly at Anneke; they'd had this conversation before. Anneke called her *boefje*, little rascal. Liesbeth was beginning an internship in a New York fashion house in January. She shared Charlotte's cigarettes and told her about a Toronto Charlotte didn't know.

—There's an exciting new clothing line, Matière Fraîche? They use things like hide and sweetgrass.

—Sweetgrass is for smudging, Charlotte said. —It must be bamboo. Or organic cotton.

–You see, she *does* know something beyond nursing! Anneke, mock-severe, lifted her eyebrows. Liesbeth patted her arm, indulging a mother's rights.

–Come for a visit while you're in New York, Charlotte found herself saying. –You can see my new house. You can meet Crofton.

–All my mother talks about is work. Are you like that?

–I'm an insomniac and I smoke too much. Among other battlefield injuries.

–You mean love affairs? said Liesbeth, and they all laughed.

She hadn't meant to tell them about the man with the pickaxe. Liesbeth gave her mother a meaningful glance. –Ma's had it too, those—hallucinations. Remember, Ma? How Pap had to take you—?

–Old houses get imprinted like that, Anneke said, shrugging. She didn't meet her daughter's glance. –It happens all the time here. He might even be watching over you, who knows?

Thomas and his brother were fighting in France, near the Belgian border. So she understood when he began visiting her at night. He had a name now, that was why he came, this eighteen-year-old with his boy's face. His battalion had been ordered to hold the line against a determined German advance south of Lille. She had a confused impression of trenches and mud, a dead horse still harnessed to a gun carriage. She woke and lay smoking with her light on, shaken, trying to catch her breath.

The next night he'd been wounded, struck by shell fragments that shredded the soft tissue in his arms. She bent over his hospital bed in her nurse's uniform. He stared at and through her, or wept uncontrollably, or told her again and again how he couldn't pull his bayonet from his enemy's body. He seemed to be recuperating at some hospital on the English coast. The voices in the dreams, at least, were English. Along with the physical injuries he had persistent diarrhoea, complete retrograde amnesia, and mutism, with a hysterical paralysis of the right arm.

On sunny days she wheeled him outside and left him sitting in the sunshine in the fresh sea air, unable to speak. She read him letters from his mother. *Dear Tom, It's been hard this year getting hands for the haying, all our lads are off serving like you, so Granddad's pitching in, imagine, and your cousins come up from over Lanark way. I've been sitting up late making over my old wedding dress for Frances, good thing she's my size! And Daisy had her litter last week, we're keeping you the runt like we promised.*

Nothing, no reaction, not a flicker.

When they could do nothing else for him they would have sent him home. His family, meeting him at the train station, would have taken him gingerly from those who'd travelled with him. A nurse, perhaps, in her blue uniform and starched white veil, a young orderly from the Medical Corps.

Did the nurse ever forget the expression on the face of Tom's mother?

When he was a little better they must have put him to work on the farm, collecting the eggs or helping lift potatoes. He sat with the hens and the young chicks for hours, holding them, talking to them softly. Regained his speech a little.

Each day he asked the same question. *When's Eddie coming home?*

What they hadn't told him in those letters, that a telegram had arrived some months earlier. Pte. Evans had been made corporal just before his death, his CO said, had distinguished himself in battle, they could be very proud of him. The battalion would be putting in for a Distinguished Conduct medal.

Soon, Tom. Very soon. Next week. Next month.

Tom was good with horses, always had been. A local dairy owner, taking pity, gave him a job in town delivering milk. Never looked you in the eye, people said, but quiet and reliable and conscientious. A good worker, even if he only talked to the animals.

At home Charlotte finished unpacking, finally, cleaned in a frenzy of intent because Anneke's daughter was coming. Crofton danced round her, bringing her his stuffed squirrel or making growling assaults on the vacuum cleaner. Amid dust and boxes and sorting she didn't notice at first that Tom had disappeared. She was perversely disappointed, then irritated, as though his visits were a duty he owed her. Perhaps he resented her alterations to the house — the remodelled bathroom, the repainted rooms.

It was January, a freezing cold January, with a dampness that bit to the bone. Bethany had gone off on a week's holiday to St. Kitts with her family, taking her course assignments with her. Under a sky pregnant with snow, Charlotte spent too much time on the internet and waited for a summons. At night, when even a handful of melatonin tablets didn't bring sleep, she re-read the old-fashioned novels of her childhood: *I Capture the Castle, The Little White Horse, A Traveller in Time.* She might be almost thirty-eight, but adulthood had eluded her. What she wanted were thick blankets and her old teddy and mugs of hot cocoa. She woke sweating out of vague nightmares in which she was running from gunfire, carrying a baby that had been entrusted to her. Ahead was a brick wall she'd have to climb, only with the child in her arms she didn't see how, and the gunfire was getting closer...

They all had it, she and Tom and Campbell, even Anneke, whatever you wanted to call it. Soldier's heart, it had been once. Did it make any difference now it had a more clinical name? One evening, out drinking with Campbell, she'd met a Canadian lieutenant-colonel who'd been a military observer in Sarajevo during the war. —Did you know, he said, what an Egyptian combat veteran wrote three thousand years ago? *Shuddering seizes you, the hair on your head stands on end, your soul lies in your hand.*

Walking back to his billet one evening, carrying a loaf of bread, he'd met a brother and sister, aged nine and eleven, out foraging for wood. He'd given them the bread, and a bar of chocolate. The next morning, in the morgue, he found their bodies, unmarked except for the sniper's bullet through each head.

Liesbeth arrived unexpectedly in the middle of a snowstorm. Her flight out of New York had been delayed, then her train out of Toronto. Charlotte, hearing the doorbell ring in the middle of the night, ran downstairs thinking of Campbell, shot in some war zone.

—So stupid of me, I erased your number! Liesbeth was

laughing on the doorstep in spite of the cold — it had dropped into the minus twenties overnight. Only her momentarily less-than-fluent English gave away her nervousness. –I am so sorry, waking you like this, I frighten you a lot, no?

Crofton, self-appointed master of ceremonies, escorted Liesbeth upstairs to the guest room, rootling through her suitcase with interested precision. In the morning she marvelled over everything: the frozen lake, the vast house, the ancient cannons across the street. She took Crofton for a walk — or he took her — and said Amsterdam, too, had once been cold enough to freeze the canals. Her grandmother remembered skating on them in winter. She even taught Crofton, in Dutch, the *sit* command, and told him solemnly how cosmopolitan he was becoming.

Charlotte took a photo of them standing in front of one of the Martello stone towers overlooking the lake. Liesbeth wore the white wool jacket with turnover collar that had won her some design competition at AMFI. Later, with Bethany, they went for drinks at the Iron Duke, where Charlotte had to explain to a bewildered Liesbeth why a Canadian pub might be named after a famous British general who had defeated Napoleon in a European battle.

Three days into Liesbeth's visit, the NGO called. A staff member had been taken ill very suddenly in Mali, could Charlotte replace him? –Stay as long as you like, she told Liesbeth, and left her preparing dinner with Bethany, who knew nothing about cooking but was learning how to make *stamppot* and *bitterballen* under Liesbeth's tutelage.

How was it you could never imagine it, flying out of a city turned the black-and-white of a Canadian winter only to land among the desert colours and withered acacia trees of a land in near-permanent drought halfway across the world? Only at night did the world she'd left behind come back to her. What filled the present was the sweat trickling beneath her uniform, the rows of cots filled with patients, the staggering exhaustion. In some other life she might be that Charlotte who led an ordinary existence. For now she was certain that any day some narrow passageway back would close and she'd be trapped here forever.

At some point he must have realized his brother wasn't coming home. Would have known, wouldn't he, without being told? And then had some argument with a stranger, a man who'd walked toward him one bright morning carrying a shovel over his shoulder. Tom, bearing his crate of milk bottles, looked up and saw — what? A German soldier coming at him with a bayonet, or so he said at his trial. It was the same soldier who'd killed his brother. That was why he'd engaged with the enemy. He spoke calmly, confidently, serene in the knowledge that he'd done his duty.

He was sentenced to life at hard labour, to be served in the federal penitentiary, less than a mile down the road from his life as a garden boy.

—We're in love, Bethany announced the day Charlotte got back from Mali.

Half-stumbling over Crofton, Charlotte set down her backpack with a thump. Straightening, she couldn't quite remember where she was.

—Liesbeth and me. An interior radiance lit Bethany up.
—I didn't tell you I was—well. You're probably not surprised,

are you? We've been phoning and texting since she left. I'm going to Amsterdam next month!

Bethany and Liesbeth? She was still in the air somewhere; a part of her hadn't caught up. *Your soul lies in your hand.* If only she could shake herself, the way Crofton did, into where she actually was.

—How marvel — I'm so happy for you, Bethany. Very happy.

To have someone who took you in their arms, who lay in bed beside you at night. What would that be like? Instead Charlotte kept intermittent company with a ghost.

—I don't know why I'm crying, I'm sorry. Bethany stood there, face wet with tears. —I'm always too emotional.

Crofton, who disapproved of emotion, especially the wet kind, was barking. Charlotte bent down and picked him up. —He's going to miss you when you're away.

—But I'm coming back! I'll bring him a gift, I'll bring him a nice new toy of his very own. Oh, Charlotte, I'm so happy!

Charlotte had driven Campbell past the penitentiary on a tour of the town's grimmer sights when he'd come to see the house. It had closed down years before, but still it made her shiver. As if the sunlight you'd been driving through a few minutes before dissolved into a dank acidic mist that didn't lift until you were on the other side. At his insistence they'd gone into the prison museum across the street, where in the gift shop he'd threatened to buy a T-shirt with *Wish you were here* printed across a barred window.

In the next room was a display of prisoners' crafts — landscape paintings, model ships, intricate knotwork. And a lifelike wooden horse, twelve inches high, carved by one Thomas Evans. Created from memory of a real horse, so the placard said, a chestnut named Diadem that had belonged to Thomas's employer. The face was remarkably expressive, alert. Dr. Streatfeild had ridden Diadem to his offices in nearby James Street for years.

He must have been a model prisoner if they'd allowed him a knife for carving. When would he have had time? On Sundays, she supposed. On the other days he would have been marched each morning through the prison gates, carrying his pickaxe on his way to work in the limestone quarry. Two lines of men in grey uniforms, those flat grey caps, forbidden to speak or gesture or even look at each other. Jeered at by small boys, pelted with stones, spoken of in dark whispers — *Look what'll happen to you if you don't do as your pa says!*

Or perhaps at night, by feel, in his tiny cell, with its cot, its Bible, its piggin of drinking water. At least until the guard came by to slam open the slot in the barred door on his hourly check.

Did his family visit on the one day they were allowed every three months? His married sister smoothing her dress, not looking at him, his mother holding herself rigid against collapse?

He came back the day after Bethany left for Amsterdam. This time he stood beneath the crabapple on her neighbour's lawn, once part of Streatfeild House's grand gardens. He still held the pickaxe, but the other hand explored the crabapple's trunk, his fingers touching its crevices. She stood watching from an upstairs window. He didn't turn to look.

He might even be watching over you, who knows. He was a virgin, she was sure of that. He had found love — in the gardens, his family, perhaps even the carving of horses — but not a lover. She would have to do. *He* would have to do, for now at least. They were stumbling through together, keeping faith with each other. What you'd gone through couldn't be ungone through. You held it at bay however you could. And sometimes you couldn't.

In bed that night, awake and smoking, she shut her eyes and summoned her first trip to Africa. The green of maize fields in the sun, the dusty dry-grass smell of the African bush, burning garbage. A small shy girl with her pet goat. The taste of grilled African pear and *suya* bought from street stalls, vendors snapping their fingers, singing out rhymes.

And the hymn they'd been singing in that little evangelical church, the women in their bright head wrappers swaying to the music, their eyes closed.

Bring down your angels, O my Lord,
All of your angels, my good Lord,
Bring them with your power and majesty,
Bring down your angels and set me free.

FIRE BREATHING

There they were. Ahead of him. Four immense black figures, curling downward at the tops, reaching out spindly crackling fingers toward him. He automatically tugged at his hose pack, but it was hopeless. −Get out! someone yelled, racing past him, −Get out, now!— *it couldn't be Ray, could it?*—*not Ray, of all people*... The nearest black figure was toppling in slow motion, if he didn't move now he'd be trapped—

He woke shouting, as always, strangling in blankets. After he'd wiped the sweat off his face he stood in the cool band of moonlight, blinds raised, staring out at an ordinary edge-of-city suburb. Out there, in the hills and mountains, the black figures walked, ever closer. It was safe, for now. Safe for as long as he and his kind did what they were trained to do—hold back the wall of flame from the world.

Over black coffee and scrambled eggs he checked his phone. No call-outs yet, just a kind of ominous silence. End of season anyway, or what used to be the end of season, though it wasn't, not anymore. November and still over a hundred active fires in the Coastal region alone. Already there'd been snow at lower levels, melted now, but that didn't mean he was done for the year. He paced, drinking a second cup. Stella bumped her nose into the back of his knee, triggering a bolt of pain. Walking her was usually Parveen's job, but she was on the other side of the planet for a wedding, some cousin or other in Chandigarh, he couldn't keep track.

You remember, Parveen would say insistently, *Kiran, the pretty one in the pink-and-gold salwar kameez, my auntie Nanda's youngest*, and he'd laugh and ask how she expected him to remember out of the fifty or sixty cousins he'd met on their honeymoon.

It was beginning to drizzle. Typical November weather for Burnaby, if you could call anything typical nowadays. He hunched into his anorak, the much-too-expensive one Parveen had bought him last Christmas, and opened the door for Stella to go arrowing out. She'd been his own present to Parveen two Christmases ago, a wriggling lump of yellow fur from a farm in Abbotsford. Black lab and golden retriever, the ad said. No, not Christmas — Diwali, when Parveen filled the house with candles and sweets and spent three days preparing a feast for their closest friends. Yes, Diwali, of course, the festival of light. That was why they'd named the puppy Stella.

—A puppy for Diwali? Parveen's brother had said in mock horror. —You are worshipping dogs now?

—Now, Dhanu. Parveen frowned at him. —Don't tease. I wanted one, you know. Ty bought me the perfect gift.

To her husband she had to explain that in parts of India people offered garlands and food to dogs and marked tikas on their foreheads during the festival. —Remember, sweetie, what I told you about dogs in Hinduism? They guard the doors of heaven and hell.

No, he hadn't. All those dizzying gods and goddesses with their multiple incarnations and avatars, their pulsating colours—how could anyone recall them all?

—My mother always said, if your pet dog sneezes while you are going out, it's a good omen, Parveen's sister-in-law added. —Remember, Dhanu, that pug of hers, how she dressed it up like a baby?

Then there was an awkward silence, because Parveen's own mother kept asking why there was no baby yet, after eight years, when Dhanu and his wife had three, all boys.

They had agreed, he and Parveen, there would never be a baby. How could you bring a baby into a world on fire?

Stella was ahead on the path to the park, growling at something. This early he hadn't bothered with the leash. —Stella! he shouted, and broke into a run. She was barking now, at what he thought was a pile of branches until it shape-shifted into a lean-to draped with a wet tarp. Under it a man, thin, aged-looking, watching Stella warily through the rain. Ty bent and grabbed her collar.

—She's harmless, just trying to be protective, he said as she twisted against his hold, giddy with bravery.

—'s'okay, the man said, except you could see it wasn't. He shook in his jean jacket, the pucker of scar on a forearm. One eye was puffy and half-shut. —You got cigarettes?

Ty didn't, so he fumbled for coins instead. The man held out a dirty palm, poked at the coins with a nicotined finger. —That all you got? He had the air of one perpetually disappointed in the human race, but he closed his fist around them. —I got something for you, eh? For luck.

He pushed a crumpled paper bag at Ty. Only when he'd walked away with Stella did he look inside. A tree cutout, one of those pine-scented things you hung in your car. He dropped it in the nearest garbage can and stooped to pick up a stick for the dog.

—Who's Ray? Parveen said when he described the dream.

—I don't know. I never knew a Ray in the crews. Not that I remember.

—Are you doing your calm breathing? He could tell she was trying hard to keep her voice level. —The way Mandy showed you?

Yes. There were days he thought it helped and days he didn't. It was one of the tools in the toolbox Mandy talked about, though a toolbox you couldn't see or touch struck him as ridiculous.

—Then call it a strategy. A technique. Parveen tightened her hands round the mug of coffee; she'd just got up. —The kids call it belly breathing.

It wasn't fair to burden her when caring for kids in pain was what she did for a living. She was a nurse in pediatric oncology, on twelve-hour shifts during weeks that always seemed to coincide with his own time off. They went to temple together occasionally; Parveen joked it was because otherwise he'd never see her. The days dedicated to Sri Ganesha, the elephant-headed god — lord of good fortune, remover of obstacles — were her favourites. There'd been a puja to the god as part of their wedding ceremony.

Ganesha had once had an ordinary human head, apparently, but his own father had replaced it with an elephant's instead out of jealousy. Parveen said the whole incident was some sort of misunderstanding. Just like all gods everywhere, forever cursing and behaving badly. He was never sure how seriously Parveen took all this, but he was happy to be with her as the tray of ghee lamps was brought round, as everyone held their hands out and brushed the light toward their eyes.

–It's taking the essence of the fire into your heart and mind, Parveen told him, which unnerved him. Did he need such essence, when he witnessed it every time he went to work?

He hoped Parveen's belief in the god who removed obstacles protected him, too.

The call-out came on Monday. Parveen wouldn't be back for another two weeks. He drove Stella to his niece's, where her eighteen-month-old and the dog could tangle together on the floor, and checked the coordinates on the status website as he headed to the airport. *Estimated size: 5 000 hectares. Suspected Cause: Person. Stage of Control: Active. Approximate Location: Binder Creek.* It had broken out on the weekend — likely a campfire — and blown up fast. An interface fire, where cabins, houses, communication lines could all be threatened. He'd fought another fire back in the summer in the same valley, only ten kilometres from this one. An evacuation order was in place, though so far it affected only two pumice mines and a hydroelectric project.

Ed, Ed Stefanovich, would be taking him up. Steady Eddie. He knew all the pilots; he'd been flying in these mountains for longer than he wanted to remember. –You got one of the Vulcan crews this time, eh? Ed said as they walked across the tarmac. —Skookum bunch of kids. Dave took em up last week.

They'd told Ty that when they called him out; all the Wildfire Service crews were on other jobs. Since his back injury the year before, when he'd been off for four long months, he'd become an itinerant crew boss, flown in on relief or wherever they needed to cobble a crew together. Vulcan had a great rep; he'd heard only good things.

—For pity's sake, Parveen said after he'd sprained his back. —Last year your shoulder, this year your lumbar. You've been doing this half your life, sweetie. You're getting too old.

But thirty-seven wasn't old. Some of the men he worked with were in their forties, even fifties, now they were calling out the retired veterans as well. The contract crews like Vulcan's were younger, mostly college kids, though fighting fires year-round meant there was more of a mix. Every year was worse than the year before. He'd still been in college, back in 2017, when the province had the worst season in its history: 1,064 fires scorching over a million hectares of forest. That twenty-year-old record had long receded, along with his plans to teach anthropology. Firefighting paid better and meant steady work.

The plane was falling through the drifting smoke, the river twisting up to meet them. As silver-grey as the cut-throat trout he'd fished for here on a field trip during his student days, when he'd worked on a pit house dig near a river tributary. They'd found a seasonal camp dating back 5,500 years. What would they think, those long-ago people, of the airborne machine that dropped humans from the sky into flame?

Ø

On a strip of pebbled beach, the helicopter was waiting for him. He and Ed high-fived and then he was dodging under the rotor blades and lifting himself into the passenger seat even as the machine rose from the ground. *Last in, last out*, he thought to himself—that was his role these days. The chopper pilot was new, some kid—younger man, he corrected himself—who grinned at him above his boom mike. They swung so low over the trees he saw a moose and her tiny calf in wetland below them. Smoke drifting across his vision erased them.

The kid—man—put the chopper down like a pro in the helispot on the hillside. Crouching, Ty scrambled out, pumping his fist when he was free of the rotors. And who was coming toward him but Graham, except it couldn't be Graham, Graham wasn't fighting fires anymore...

—Hey Ty, I'm Reid, they said you were coming up. Dad says to say hi.

And the boy who'd been born in the middle of the Sicamous fire stuck his hand out, laughing Graham's body-shaking laugh. That had been Ty's second summer fighting fires on Graham's crew. Graham hadn't seen his son until he was two weeks old.

—Dad says you're among the best because he trained you himself. That laugh again, and the teasing, what they called fire-bagging.

A clump of burning debris landed at their feet. —Fire whirls already? Ty said, and glanced automatically uphill.

—Yeah, things picked up this morning, we're getting crossover conditions, weird this time of year, huh?

Not just weird but impossible. Who'd ever heard of it in BC in November?

∅

He'd met a First Nations firekeeper on that student field trip, an elder who sat silent while her son talked. Their family had been firekeepers for thousands of years, the son told the dig team. —Lines of our people walked the land beating drums. We warned the birds and the four-leggeds.

That was their hereditary role, to renew and purify the land through fire. —My mother taught us that every fire is like a snowflake. No two are alike.

Every fire is like a snowflake. Yes. Each fire was a live thing with a mind of its own. Fire was a divine attribute, after all, a gift of the gods, or else it was stolen from them and the thief punished. It wasn't something you messed around with. But they'd thought themselves able to control it, white people had. They'd suppressed it for hundreds of years, and now it rose up against them, blisteringly intense, full of fury.

The Vulcan team was working in four sub-crews that day. He didn't meet them all until their shifts ended. Five women, the rest guys, though he soon lost track of their names.

—Got slimed today pretty bad, one of them—Mike?— said when the first crew came into spike camp that evening. His chest heaved in spasm, choking his words.

—Here, have some Vitamin I, Veronica said, sliding the ibuprofen bottle across the counter as the others laughed. They were at ease; they'd had a good day, a good pull, despite the fire retardant. Some people were more reactive than others, though nothing like the borate salts they'd used when he was the age of these kids. Gave you runs so bad you were pissing liquid shit for days.

—Black coffee does it for me, Reid said. —Honest. Opens up the airway.

—How'd you learn that already, snookie? said Jai. —Second year on crew and he thinks he knows it all, eh?

Ty left them to the banter to find his cot and fall into comatose sleep, though not before trying, and failing, to get a signal so he could phone Parveen. Not that she'd be surprised if he didn't. You couldn't count on it out here. Besides, she was in that other dimension half a world away, helping choose the music, the jewellery, the *lehenga choli* the bride would wear. There—he'd remembered something about Parveen's universe after all.

On the second day he found himself in a sub-crew with Reid at the perimeter, digging a firebreak. The weather had changed, bringing rain squalls and sleet. They could focus on tactical work, get ahead a bit, though his hands had numbed with cold. Every time he turned and looked at Reid he saw Graham, that same sunburst of freckles over his nose. If it wasn't for the flickering pain in his lower back he'd have felt years younger.

—Don't do this forever, he told Reid as he straightened against a muscle spasm. —Don't trash your body like I did.

—Oh, I'm a goner, Reid said. —Anyway, you and Dad did.

—Yeah, and now your dad's wearing a truss and his rotator cuff's shot.

The muscle seized again but he was already over the limit for ibuprofen. —How's he doing these days? He couldn't remember the last time he'd seen Graham, now in a desk job at headquarters in Parksville.

—Bored, Reid said, and laughed, and whacked at the ground with his pulaski. —Tells me how he envies me.

Well, the old always did, didn't they? Envy the young? If Ty had married early, like Graham, maybe he'd have chosen parenthood after all, have a son like Reid. Another would-be lifer, in love with gut-wrenching challenge. In love with fire, really, and the outdoors, and the trees themselves.

They weren't always menacing and spindly fingered, the trees in his dreams. In the last year or two things had changed. He had no idea why. That first time, he was in a northern forest with his hand on the white bark of a paper birch. Three eyelike knots stared back at him. The tree was trying to tell him something, and he stood there listening. The voice was brisk, eager, impatient. He was on the edge of understanding, but he couldn't quite make it out. He woke into sheets damp with sweat, but from exertion, not fear. He lay still, puzzling, for a long time.

Spruce came some months later, slow of speech and rather condescending. A black spruce, from those same northern forests where so much had burned in the last decade. This tree was young, not much more than a sapling, and the new growth of fireweed frothed around it. Every sound was intense: a downy woodpecker rapping on a nearby trunk, a ground squirrel chittering alarm. The spruce took its time, leaning toward him as if blown by high wind. Ty wondered if it was because he hadn't been able to keep up with the birch. The woodpecker's rapping was a message too, but he was too slow, too stupid. He looked down at his trenching tool and threw it away, and then he woke.

On the fourth day the clouds blew off and the ground began drying under a sudden blast of sun. A breakout on the hillside above them was radioed in from a bird dog. A smouldering hotspot, maybe. Ty dispatched a sub-crew that included Reid and went back to trenching.

Fifteen minutes later a call came in: Veronica, her breath ragged. They needed more personnel, fast. —We're back into a Rank 3, she said.

That meant open flame, the tops of trees torching. Jesus. He headed up himself with his sub-crew and another. Harder to breathe now, the smoke thickening as they climbed, their voices hollowed. The trees around them seemed to buckle in the waves of heat. A couple of his crew ran past, yanking on their hose packs. Already the flames were soaring up a hundred metres or more, the wind egging them on. Had he miscalculated? Half the hillside was jackstrawed pine, beetle-killed, which meant much greater fire intensity with the right conditions. And even wet weather didn't dampen ground fuel these days.

He was lightheaded and his back twinged but he plunged on. A young doe leapt past him, ears flat with fear. He yanked out his radio phone and called in the bambi bucket and hoped—*christ*—it wasn't too late.

He'd met the god of fire at their wedding ceremony. He and Parveen made the traditional seven circles around the altar with its consecrated flames so that Agni could witness their vows. The god had two heads and seven tongues and rode on a ram, holding an axe and a torch. When he died in the myths he was dismembered, his flesh and fat turned into resin, his bones into pine trees. He could be resurrected only by new fire, just as the lodgepole pines that blazed around Ty on the hillsides needed fire to regenerate. Only in the intense heat of a wildfire would their cones open and drop their seeds.

They tamped it down, but only just. For the rest of the day he pulled his crew from one spot to another, helped build a firebreak for half a dozen cabins, liaised with the helitack crew that brought in equipment. The chopper brought in more fire crew as well, and flew out a rookie overcome with smoke inhalation. It was almost midnight when Ty got back to the spike camp. Only Veronica was there. Stiff, stunned, he heaped cold pasta on a plate in the kitchen.

—You want a Coke or something? she said as he lowered himself to a chair. She passed him a can. —You don't know when to quit, do you?

—You ever been a crew boss? he said, mouth half-full.

—As a matter of fact, yeah. On the big Yukon fires back in '33. She ran a hand across a face lined with dirt and exhaustion. —Fires are changing. Everything about them's changing. And the way to fight them.

—We should have called in the stitch drop sooner, is that it?

—I remember when we were up near Dawson. The rotor wash threw embers into the green, I'd never seen it catch so fast. We jumped out and started digging fireline. There were full minutes when I thought, this may be it, we may not make it.

She was talking about this fire, earlier that day, he was sure. *Every fire is like a snowflake.* She was wrong, and also right, and she wasn't shy about it. He'd pushed too hard to come back to work, probably. It was like a drug: the adrenaline, the thrill of victory.

—I'm going to try and catch some sleep, he said, and tipped the rest of the pasta in the garbage.

He'd read about firefighters who deliberately started fires. Not that the Wildfire Service ever said as much. It got classified under Cause: Person. He understood it, in a strange way. Firefighters and fire were locked together in an embrace, a chokehold, and who were you if you didn't have fires to fight? Better than sitting at home waiting for a call-out, pacing. Funny how easy it would be to start one, how difficult to control. They started deliberate fires all the time to create a line of fire as a firebreak. The modern-day version of the fire god wore a Nomex suit, held a driptorch in one hand and a pulaski in the other. You fought and pulled back, created and destroyed.

It was still only 20 percent contained when he was pulled off after a nineteen-day stint of thirty-six-hour shifts and sent home. He needed a break, even he knew that, and Parveen was back, and he wanted to see her. She picked him up at the airport, Stella bouncing with delirium in the back seat. He left a smudge on Parveen's cheek from the grime still under his fingernails. As always she was the one talking on the way home; he stared out the window at the green lawns, the drizzle spotting the windshield.

—I've got a surprise for you, she told him as they pulled into the driveway. Stella, barking, leapt out and chased a robin across the grass.

–My favourite dinner?

That would be *murg makkai* with Parveen's special filled naan, and basmati rice, and mango ice cream for dessert.

–I'm pregnant.

He couldn't have heard right. The flames still roared in his ears. But Parveen's tremulous smile, shy and startled and overcome—

–Really, Ty. I went to the doctor yesterday. Mami said she thought I was and the doctor confirmed it.

As in a dream he put his arms around her and she collapsed in tears against his shoulder, then pulled back and brushed them away, half-laughing. –So silly of me, I don't know what is the matter. She was falling back into the Punjabi syntax he'd found so charming when they were dating. –And you've only just arrived and look, I just dump this news on you. Let's go in, darling, you're exhausted.

–When—when's he—?

–Late July, the doctor says. Around the twenty-fifth or so, but of course it's not exact. And it could be a girl, you know. They can't do an ultrasound before the twelfth week.

He watched Parveen moving around the kitchen, talking about a nursery, about telling his parents, and felt a sudden bloom of protectiveness, a fierce need to shelter her. This wasn't supposed to happen, but it had. He supposed they'd been careless. Overconfident. Like him with the fire a few days ago.

–This is—you're okay with this? she said suddenly, the rice cooker paused in midair. –I didn't ask about—you know, at the doctor's. I couldn't. Not when Mami knew.

She was looking down at the pot in her hands, not at him. It had all been decided without him, for him. In the last couple of months there'd been four deaths on her pediatric unit, four children under ten. Something in her had wanted balance, restoration. And maybe the spruce sapling...? But that was crazy. He was just tired. Overwhelmed.

His first night home it was, apparently, the turn of a lodge-pole pine to come to him. Unusually tall, singed by an old lightning strike, with missing branches on its lower half and near the top a burst of the witches' broom caused by rust fungus. It was old, this tree, old and slow and full of wisdom—appropriate for a species that had been around for millions of years. He touched the cone buds at the tips of the branches and felt a shock of electricity, and then a knowing. Nothing he could put into words, but a freeing, a lightness, an opening up in his chest. First Nations people had used pine needle tea against colds and sore throats, he remembered from somewhere. The conelet—in the way of dreams he had swallowed it—expanded and opened in the heat of his own body, and for the first time in years he woke without a headache.

He was called back on a relief crew a week later, working again with Reid and a Vulcan team. The fire was contained on its eastern flank but not the west, where spot fires had started. Temperatures in the area had gone up to thirty-two degrees Celsius. In early January. He didn't startle, as he once would have, when an olive-sided flycatcher flew overhead as he was washing up in camp the first evening. So many birds that used to migrate in winters no longer did. In the kitchen he ate mechanically, thinking of Parveen, of the baby—the size of a sweet pea, so the doctor said.

—How's Sweet Pea? he said when he called.

—Not very sweet. Still making me sick in the mornings.

But some women got worse morning sickness than Parveen did, so he'd been told. One of the older crew members said his wife had spent much of the first eight weeks of each pregnancy in bed. His mother-in-law claimed it was a good omen; the baby was full of vigour. Parveen herself said the baby would be a Leo, one of the fire signs.

—So it must be all your fault! she'd said, pinching his chin.

Half the crew were fighting colds. Reid was living, so he said, on oil of oregano. —My girlfriend's into all these health things, he said, and swallowed a slug of the oil, grimacing. —She says it's a natural antibiotic. Good for my gut, too.

—In my day it was beer. Ty shoulder-punched him, gently.

—Weren't you telling me just the other day not to trash myself? Reid punched back, grinning. —This way we're gonna live forever, you know that? Meanwhile his dad was still raring to go, if they let him. —I swear he's got a bag packed ready and waiting. Mom's choked, she doesn't want two of us fighting fires.

It wasn't fighting anymore so much as living with. Ty had understood that much, at least, from the pine. Fire was an ally, not an enemy. It could never be fully contained. You danced with it up the mountain and down again. More and more fires were allowed to burn now; there simply weren't the resources to fight them. This one, the Binder Creek fire, was threatening several small communities, and the air quality health index was off the scale.

On the fifth day he was working downslope, building yet another firebreak to prevent the fire jumping the creek.

It had consumed over a hundred thousand hectares now, engulfing an abandoned gold and copper mine known to be leaking toxins. They had to wear face masks, though Ty hated them; they made it difficult to breathe. Ahead of him, upslope, Gord was working with the chainsaw, falling insect-deadened pine, with Reid and Jai following behind with their pulaskis, digging down to mineral soil. Using hand signals to communicate because radio didn't always work in this terrain. An extended horizontal thumb meant go back, two fingers in a horizontal V meant keep your eyes on the green.

Ty had his head down, hacking with his own tool, when he heard shouts above the roar of the fire. One of the crew had five fingers flashing open and shut: an accident. Farther up the hill other crew were hosing down a burning tree that lay horizontal. Ty started up toward it at an awkward run. Now he could see a streak of yellow jacket underneath it, and Gord with his chainsaw bucking the top of the tree. His heart cratered into his stomach. Dear god, let it not be Reid. Already he saw himself on the phone, having to tell his old friend Graham...

But it *was* Reid, the blackened trunk diagonal across his chest and shoulder, eyes glassy with pain. Breathing, thank god, still breathing as Ty and the others worked to free him. Deanna, the line medic, brought up a traverse rescue stretcher and stabilized his upper body before they moved him.

—Fast as a lightning bolt, that top snapping out.

They stood watching, Ty and Gord, as the stretcher was carried downhill to the evacuation site. Gord pressed his fingers in his eye sockets, face white under the dirt layer.

—I shoulda seen him. He was in the danger zone under the lean.

Ty rested a hand on Gord's shoulder, half-turned to look back up the slope at the fallen tree. He'd just been through a safety review with the crew about burning snags. Lots of times you never saw them coming. Every tree was different. How rotten, how much of it was burning, how long it had burned. You never knew.

He worked the rest of the day with a sharp pain in his chest that wasn't from the smoke. That evening his radio crackled in its holster. Reid had broken an arm and his collarbone and punctured a lung, but he was stable, in intensive care in Vancouver. His parents and younger sister had flown over from the Island. Reid had asked a buddy at Vulcan to be sure and call Ty.

He felt the tears come then. Had to sit, or rather give way, onto a nearby stump, pull his mask off and squeeze the liquid out of his eyes. *Getting soft, old man. Get a grip for christ sake.* He pulled his mask back down shakily and stood, leaning on his trenching tool until he got his breath back.

Reid was back at work within three months, or so Ty heard. Telling people he'd nearly bought it and that the best thing was to get back in the saddle. Had he learned anything at all? Only that he'd survived through blind, dumb luck. You couldn't plan for it, couldn't alter what you did, except develop that sixth sense Ty himself now had. It had saved him from death more than once. That and being humble in the face of a devouring beast that showed no mercy. The beast itself would teach him, in the end. Nothing else.

The fire was contained by then only because of heavy wet snow. With the crews pulled off he was in waiting mode again, sitting at home, teaching Stella the *stay* position, to come when called. Sweet Pea had turned visible, an egglike bulge in Parveen's stomach, pressing insistently against the waistband of her nursing outfit. They hadn't wanted to know the gender after the ultrasound.

—Mami says I shouldn't wear white anymore, Parveen told him. She stood in the kitchen stirring turmeric and chiles into sizzling onion. He brushed by Sweet Pea — the face? a leg? — as he took knives and forks to the table.

—It's the colour of mourning in India, you know, only widows wear white. Silly, isn't it. Anyway I said I'd go shopping with her. Blue or pink, what do you think?

She was teasing, her eyes sparking. Waving the chef's knife around as she began dancing bhangra fashion. Stella, always wanting to be part of everything, made little rushes at Parveen's bare feet. Parveen pulled Ty back into the kitchen to dance with her until the shrilling smoke alarm told them the onions were burning.

He was home for five weeks, the longest break he'd had for reasons other than injury in years. They cleaned out what had been, variously, an office, a den, a sewing room. Repainted, installed a crib, a comfortable armchair, a changing table. There was no need to shop for baby clothes; his mother-in-law was round every week with new items. He read articles online about bringing a new baby home to a house with a dog. There could be jealousy issues. *Introduce your dog to smells like baby lotion and powder. Bring an item from the hospital that contains your baby's scent before the homecoming.*

They talked about names. Stewart Amar, after his grandfather and Parveen's; Brighid, after the Celtic goddess of fire and poetry (Ty's mother's suggestion) and Simran, after Parveen's mother. Simran meant remembrance or meditation. Parveen was carrying a girl, so her mother insisted; she'd consulted an astrologer. Really, the child should be named based on her *jyotiṣa* chart, which could not be cast until the exact date and time of birth.

A few days later, out with Stella in the park, Ty threw a stick that arced into a bush next to a pine tree. As Stella wrestled with retrieval, he stared at the pine with the shock of familiarity. The same lightning singe as the one in his dream, the same missing branches, the burst of fungus. The conelet in his chest expanded again, making it difficult to breathe. The scent of pine was overwhelming. He had to lock his knees to stop them trembling. His mind groped for logic. He must, surely, have seen the pine before the dream. But the trail he was on was new to him, recently cut and cedar-chipped.

Perhaps five weeks off wasn't long enough after all. The arrival of the child, this world-changing event... And all those injuries over the years, what they'd done to his body. And his mind.

He whistled Stella back, turned away.

But when the call-out came Ty went, of course. That was what you did. This time in the southeast of the province, mercifully not near assets. Late March and bone-dry, what with the drought of the last two years. The fire was in a valley, working its way upslope. They'd dropped in smokejumpers earlier; he was in a mop-up crew. He wondered, briefly, why they hadn't called him sooner. He hadn't jumped in years, but surely he could have been on a ground team or at base camp. Though really he didn't want that. He wanted to be at the fire face, studying what he now thought of not as an enemy but a teacher. Some ancient and relentless teacher who gave no quarter. Just as in martial arts, you had to use the fire's own strength against it.

He was summoned back to base late one afternoon. No reason given, just a terse radio call. —Fill you in when you get here, his supervisor said. Some new task, some new set of operational commands. Sometimes they made sense, but more often he chafed, knowing he'd mainly rely on his gut to keep him and his crew safe. He didn't cut corners, he wasn't a risk taker that way, but you had to let your body, with its knowledge that was now second nature, lead.

His wife's brother had phoned; he was to call right away. His heart did a backflip into the gut he'd been exalting. It took nearly three hours to get a signal. He sat praying—to what he didn't know—for only the second time in his life.

—I am so sorry, Ty, Dhanu said, close to tears, when Ty finally got hold of him. —It is Parveen, she is—how do I say this?—

—What? She's—what? He was almost incoherent with terror.

—The baby, it is the baby. Dhanu choked on a sob. —She lost the baby.

Ø

There was no night flight crew available to fly him home. And it wasn't a matter of life and death — not his own, at least. Parveen was okay, Dhanu said — sedated, in a private room, her mother or one of her nursing friends with her. The hospital had offered grief counselling. Ty heard and didn't hear. *She was safe, Parveen, as long as she was safe* ... But out of the roil in his mind, in his body, toward morning Sweet Pea floated clear. She had her mother's small flared nose and his own mother's bowlike mouth. Her eyes were closed, her fist against her cheek. In the smoky air of the tent he might have reached out and touched her.

We travel with you, the pine said. *We have entered you.*

–But Parveen, he said, swallowing a sob. –If I'd been home more — I was away so much...

You were called away. You obeyed the call. What has happened is not in your power to alter.

He must have slept after all, because when he opened his eyes it was the grey-dark of imminent day. The dawn chorus was starting — a couple of varied thrushes, a ruby-crowned kinglet. He rolled over and stood, his hand going automatically to the deep spasms in his lower back. In the pain he felt a kind of ridiculous comradeship with Parveen. More birds now, joining up, dropping in and out, swelling into throbbing intolerable life. *Shut up, shut up,* he thought, and wept, softly. He found he was cradling his arms for the child, and he held her until the sun rose, through the morning singing, until he couldn't any longer.

HOLDING
PATTERNS

THE CALLIGRAPHER'S DAUGHTER

It was the fourth day of Ramadan and the calligrapher's daughter sat, as she always did, with her *qalams* of sharpened reed, her inks of soot and copper sulphate bound with wine, her burnished paper. From the kitchen came her sisters' chatter and the smell of *harira*, the dish that would break their fast that evening. As the youngest she ought to be among them, chopping and stirring, measuring and tasting, but the calligrapher's daughter was exempt from such chores. From the age of two, when she had traced, with her finger, the whorls and flourishes of her father's manuscripts, he had treated her as his apprentice. He taught her how to hold the pen, gave her scraps of paper on which to practise. –Look! he had said then. –She is in love, as I was! Her sisters muttered to each other about sorcery, enchantment, other dark spells. –She is the pearl of my old age, their father answered. And when people said –*Lesou alhaz*, what a misfortune, the calligrapher has only daughters, he replied –Allah, praise be unto Him, has consoled me with a daughter with talent.

At seven the calligrapher's daughter was writing letters for her neighbours. At twelve she began transcribing her first Qur'an. At fourteen she received her first commission: a suite of poems by the magnificent fourteenth-century Grenadine poet Ibn al-Khatib, to be transcribed on gazelle's vellum and presented as a wedding gift from a Fez princeling to his bride. When not working she spent hours in her father's library, which held a Qur'an that was said to have once belonged to the great Baghdad scholar Ya'qūb ibn Ishāq al-Kindī. Its pages were stained with salt and ocean spray, its binding frayed, but merely to hold it, or so the calligrapher's daughter believed, was to feel inspiration from the Divine Radiance flowing into one's fingers. Its anonymous creator, whoever she was — for the calligrapher's daughter was certain it was a woman — deserved, of course, no credit, as her father had long ago taught her. All credit belonged to Allah, who had sent the Qur'an to humankind as a talisman of the Hidden Book known only to the Lord of the Worlds Himself. For, as the Qur'an said —*If all the trees in the earth were pens, and if the sea eked out by seven seas more were ink, the Words of God could not be written out to the end.*

Now, on the fourth day of Ramadan, the calligrapher's daughter was beginning the most important commission she had ever undertaken — that of a Qur'an for the sultan himself. It was to be a gift from the grand vizier of the court, to be presented three months hence on the fifth anniversary of the sultan's victory over the Portuguese at the battle of Ksar el-Kebir, when he had vanquished five hundred ships and eighteen thousand men, with nine thousand dead and the rest taken prisoner. An almost impossible period of time in which to complete the work, yet it was difficult to concentrate with her stomach gurgling from hunger. The calligrapher's daughter picked up one of her pens, dipped it into the pot of powdered gold ink, and began drawing an arabesque within one of the *shamsahs*, the little suns that illuminated the margins. While she worked it was as though her father sat beside her, guiding her hand, murmuring instructions about the pressure of the pen, the angle of the nib, the purity of the letters.

–Handwriting, he had told her when she was still small, is jewellery by the hand from the pure gold of the intellect. It is also brocade woven by the reed pen with the thread of understanding. He himself was too old, now, to do the work—his hand shook, his sight had dimmed—but every day he came to inspect her own, to hold it up against the light that entered through the narrow window.

–Yes, daughter, here on this page you have achieved perfection, he would say. –The perfection, that is, that Allah allows us to claim, though all our work is imperfect compared to His.

Sometimes he took a pen and deliberately marred one of the still-wet letters, making her cry out; she couldn't help it.

–Perfection is for Allah only, he always said. –Let us remain humble by never forgetting.

–Handwriting may be jewellery and brocade, her sister Sa'aida said, but when the time comes I want my wedding dress woven of real silk, not words. Even if they are from the Qur'an.

A statement that had scandalized everyone else, though the calligrapher's daughter merely smiled. Wedding dresses, no matter how finely woven, fell apart, but the words of the Qur'an lasted forever.

∅

At sunset every day the calligrapher's daughter laid aside her pens and joined her family for the evening meal. The others laughed, recounted the latest gossip, teased each other, but the calligrapher's daughter sat silent, filled with the words she had been transcribing.

–Another serving, sister? her eldest sister said, and added mockingly –Even *you* cannot live on words alone.

Afterwards the calligrapher's daughter returned to her table and worked by lamplight far into the night. Her father cautioned her against spoiling her eyes, but the truth was she had no choice if she was to complete the task in the time allowed. She prayed for a steady hand and a pure heart. One could not rush, especially when transcribing the very words that the angel Jibra'il had revealed to the Prophet, peace be upon him. Still, human deadlines—and especially those of a sultan—had also to be respected. Besides, the household depended on her earnings, now that her oldest sister was a widow and the husband of the second-oldest was ill. Apart from her four sisters and two brothers-in-law there were eight grandchildren, the youngest a mere few weeks old. She had a feeling about this youngest, a girl named Maryam after her grandmother. The calligrapher's daughter could already see, in the baby's fat fingers, the potential for holding a *qalam* as though she had been born for nothing else.

On the nineteenth day of Ramadan, after sunset, the grand vizier himself paid a call. His arrival sent all the women into a frenzy of preparation. Tea must be made and served in the ornate pot kept for special guests, sweetmeats chosen and set out on a tray, the vizier's horse stabled, his servants given something to eat. The calligrapher's daughter heard all the commotion outside but paid no attention. She had long ago learned to resist the temptation of the streets. She continued working steadily even when the grand vizier entered the room, accompanied by her father leaning on his staff.

—No, no, the grand vizier said as her father, scandalized, urged her to cover her face and rise. —I see she is hard at work, and the deadline is short. He bent over the table and scrutinized the page she was working on, where the heading of Surah 68, "The Pen," was enclosed in a glowing rectangle of gold, crimson, and blue.

—Magnificent, he murmured. —Truly, you are guided by the hand of Allah, as Zayd ibn Thābit himself must have been.

There was no greater compliment than to be compared to the Scribe of the Prophet. The calligrapher's daughter bowed her head as her father said —Really, your honour, you are too kind, much too kind. My daughter is young still, she has not come into her full powers, she—

—Then she will astound the world when she does, the grand vizier said sharply, and turned on his heel. At the door he said —An extra hundred gold *benduqi* if you can complete it a week early. I should like to have it displayed at the palace for all to see.

—An extra hundred *benduqi*! her father muttered after the vizier was gone. —The man cannot be a true Muslim to speak so. Perhaps he is a convert.

The calligrapher's daughter said nothing, but a quiet pride filled her. She must be careful, she knew, not to let such praise go to her head. Still, it was gratifying to receive such approval when she was still young enough to savour the sweetness. Her father had been well into middle age before receiving his rightful due for his skills. –What a shame, one of her sisters had said then, that Allah sends almonds to those without teeth.

The completed Qur'an was indeed delivered early to the vizier. It was presented to the sultan in an elaborate ceremony, to which the calligrapher's daughter, as a woman, was not invited. The next day it was displayed on a silk cushion on a marble table in one of the visiting rooms of the palace, and thousands lined up to see it. A messenger in a glittering turban arrived on horseback at the calligrapher's house, bearing a purse with one hundred *benduqi* in it in addition to the fee the calligrapher's daughter had already been promised. She gave the money to her father for distribution to the household, retaining for herself only enough to buy new pens and more copper sulphate.

A week later another messenger arrived. He bore a scroll with the sultan's seal on it, addressed to the calligrapher's daughter herself, commanding her to appear at the palace after Friday prayers. The calligrapher's daughter re-rolled the scroll with trembling fingers. What was the purpose of this command, addressed to her, a mere scribe, and a woman at that? Had her work displeased the sultan after all? He was known to be capricious, mercurial, someone who did not suffer fools gladly. The palace, so it was said, held three hundred and fifty rooms, lavishly decorated with ivory, gems, and cedar wood, a pool made of Italian marble and gold, and vast gardens where fountains played. And also an underground tunnel leading to a jail where thousands of prisoners were held captive.

On Friday a troop of the sultan's own royal guard arrived

to escort her to the palace. Her sisters, who had helped choose the kaftan she was to wear, trilled and fluttered, but the calligrapher's daughter thought only of how she might never see them again. She squeezed little Maryam tightly and bent low over her father's hand.

—A great honour, my daughter, her father murmured, though she thought she caught a flicker of anxiety in his voice. She took with her her pens and inks and paper, in case his majesty commanded her to write something there and then.

At the palace she was led through room after room, each more dazzling than the last. She was almost dizzy with its splendours when she was shown into a small alcove hidden behind a plain curtain. There, seated on a cushion on the floor, was a man dressed in a simple brown djellaba, a Qur'an open in front of him on a cushion. Could this really be the sultan? He motioned her to a low stool nearby. The calligrapher's daughter sank onto it, trembling.

—I come here daily, the sultan told her, to remind myself that I am a mere servant of Allah, like other mortals, though I rule a sultanate and own five thousand slaves. I come to be reminded of the Knower of All, Whose mysteries have no end. And the first mystery is this: Why did the Hidden One give such power as you possess to a woman?

—Your majesty, the calligrapher's daughter stammered, but the sultan waved a hand.

—Of course you do not know. Only the Knower knows. Then tell me this: Why is it that the Qur'an you prepared, all honour be to the Glorious One, dazzles me so much I cannot look at it?

Again the calligrapher's daughter found herself stammering.

–I keep it on a lectern by my bed, the sultan went on. –And when I wake in the night, it glows with a strange light, and the letters blaze like letters of fire. Who taught you such craft?

The calligrapher's daughter stared at him, unable to answer. The Qur'an, in her own humble estimation, was certainly the most beautiful she had ever made, blasphemy though it might be to think so, yet in her own hands it had never glowed and blazed in the way the sultan described.

–Perhaps, she finally murmured, what you are seeing is a pale reflection of the Light Itself, your majesty.

The sultan was silent for a long time. –Last night, he said slowly, this is the surah that blazed out at me: *If someone kills another person — unless in retaliation for someone else or for causing corruption in the earth — it is as if he had murdered all mankind. And if anyone gives life to another person, it is as if he had given life to all mankind.* The sultan raised his eyes. –Tell me, was it you who arranged that this surah should be emphasized above all others?

The calligrapher's daughter was so terrified she couldn't speak. She shook her head and opened her mouth, but nothing came out.

–I see you have brought your instruments with you, the sultan said softly. –I will have a room prepared for you where you may work. You will be my guest until you can answer my question.

Her family understood her new situation to be the greatest of honours. The calligrapher's daughter, however, understood that she was a prisoner, even if her cell was the most luxurious room she had ever seen. What answer could she give the sultan? If a certain surah blazed like fire, that was the will of Allah — it had nothing to do with her. Perhaps the sultan's guilty conscience was driving him mad. Perhaps the souls of the many who had died in battle hovered round him at night, erupting into his dreams.

The calligrapher's daughter sat at her desk day after day, with her pens and inks and paper, but her talent seemed to have deserted her. Either she smeared the ink, or she chose the wrong pen, or the paper itself seemed to resist her. She tried prayer and rest and fasting. Nothing worked. She took to walking in the palace gardens, among the groves of lemon and myrtle, the cooing of doves and the splash of the fountains. She saw arabesques in the grapevines, and dazzling *shamsahs* if she glanced upward at the sun. Perhaps the praise had gone to her head after all, and she was being reminded that the Shaper of Beauty Himself was in charge, not her. Hadn't He created the first pen, after all, and commanded it to write?

She was sitting by a fountain one day when she saw a figure dressed in white strolling through a grape arbour in the distance. As the figure came closer she saw it was a man — a Christian, no less, judging by the green fleur-de-lys cross embroidered on his white mantle. He could only be one of the sultan's prisoners. She flung her veil across her face, a movement that must have attracted his attention, because he started and then bowed low.

—My apologies, your highness, for intruding on your solitude here. The sun was in my eyes, I failed to see you. He bowed again and began to withdraw, but the calligrapher's daughter put out a hand.

–You are not intruding at all, sir. Nor am I a member of the royal court. I am a prisoner, like you.

The man — young and fair-haired and bearded in the Christian manner — stared at her.

–*You*, your highness? He spoke Arabic surprisingly well, though with an accent. –But you ... He looked about him, as if for assistance.

–I am a calligrapher. I was commissioned to produce a — she hesitated at the thought of pronouncing the name of the Divine Book in an infidel's presence — a gift for the sultan. Unfortunately I displeased him. So here I am.

–And I — the Christian again gave one of those peculiar bows — I am Frei João Álvares of the Knights of St. Benedict of Avis, taken prisoner in battle on the fourth of August, 1578. He gave a huge sigh, and the calligrapher's daughter fancied that she saw the glitter of tears in his eyes. –The one where our young king himself was slain, God have mercy on his soul.

As he crossed himself, his head bent, the calligrapher's daughter averted her face and spoke to the myrtle hedge. –Surely, sir, your compatriots will ransom you?

–The Portuguese treasury has been emptied in our attempts to ransom all the prisoners, Frei João Álvares replied wearily. –My own hopes must rest instead on my fellow knights, and on Our Lord and Saviour, whom I serve.

The calligrapher's daughter shuddered. Still, the Prophet himself, peace be upon him, had urged that all peoples of the Book be treated with respect, even if they chose to ignore the latest revelation. This man had been a prisoner for over five years. He might never see his native land again.

–Your sultan has been most gracious, Frei João Álvares

went on. —He allows me to worship in my own way and to have the full use of his libraries, which contain many Christian books. But all I wish for is the sight of the spires of Santa Maria Maior towering over the roofs of Lisbon, where I will give thanks to the Virgin for my safe deliverance.

But surely this handsome young man had a wife whom he also missed? Frei João Álvares smiled. —I am a friar. A kind of— He floundered about for the right word in Arabic. —I have taken vows of poverty, chastity, piety, and obedience. I serve only God and Christ.

The calligrapher's daughter had heard of this peculiar habit of Christians, that of celibacy. Such a renunciation of joy could only have been devised by men who worshipped a man nailed to a cross. Still, deluded as he was, this man's future, like her own, depended on the whim of the sultan. They might have been two flies trapped together in a spider's web.

—You have been most gracious, Frei João Álvares said, but I am wearying you with my misfortunes. Let me, in recompense, ask if I might bring you a book from the sultan's library. Some light reading, perhaps, that will help pass the time—

The calligrapher's daughter stared at the ground at her feet. She had no wish for anything but the Qur'an itself.

—Surely there is something I can bring you, Frei João Álvares said.

—Perhaps... She hesitated, not wishing to have the sultan's attention drawn to her. —Yes, she said at last, boldly, there *is* something. If I might see the famous Pearl Qur'an they say the sultan's ancestors brought with them when they were expelled from Al-Andalus...

There—she had said it. She wondered if Frei João Álvares would object, but he merely bowed again. —As you wish, he said. —I will request the sultan's permission.

This time the sun was in the eyes of the calligrapher's daughter, and when she looked again he had disappeared.

Permission came a few days later, in the form of a note written by the sultan's secretary and delivered on a silver tray incised with gold. The note ordered her to follow the slave who brought it. He guided her through the many rooms of the palace to a separate wing, where two guards stood at attention in front of huge doors made of cedar, carved with peacocks and birds of paradise. One of the guards unlocked the doors with a massive key fastened to his belt and swung them wide.

The calligrapher's daughter stood dumbfounded. Stretching away into the distance were row upon row of shelves, each one rising from floor to ceiling, containing what must be thousands of books and scrolls and manuscripts. A domed ceiling of azure sat above it all like a lid on a sugar bowl, only the sweetness this bowl held was for the eyes and the mind. Half-dazed, the calligrapher's daughter stepped across the threshold. Surely she was dreaming. She wandered up and down the shelves, not daring to touch anything.

At last she came to the section that held religious treatises, including several illuminated Qur'ans under lock and key. On a nearby table an old leather case had been set out on a cushion, a magnifying glass and a wooden page-turner beside it, evidently for her use. She sat down reverently. —*Subhanallah*, she muttered under her breath, and opened the case.

From the first glorious pages to the last, she had never beheld such a magnificent Qur'an. Written in the Maghrebi script of Al-Andalus, it was both familiar and strangely exotic, bringing tidings of a lost world that must have been much closer to God. Whether it was the quality of the ink or the smoothness of the paper or the richness of the ornamentation, the calligrapher's daughter did not know, only that no one in her own fallen age could ever produce a Qur'an like this one. She turned the pages in increasing despair. What was the point of her own work, compared to this? When she came to the last page she closed the book gently, returned it to its case with infinite care, and stumbled out of the library.

The sun had set, but the calligrapher's daughter barely noticed. Nor did she notice the magnificence of the rooms as she was led back to her own, where she threw herself on her divan. Clearly her life was over. There was no point in being a calligrapher when the most exquisite Qur'an ever created by human hands already existed. But if she wasn't a calligrapher, what was she?

She had lived for naught. She was being punished twice over for her overweening pride. She lay tearless in the darkness, too anguished even to mutter one of the Ninety-Nine Names of Allah.

All the next day she sat in the gardens, where the lemon trees had lost their colour and the fountains had turned to ash. Toward evening she heard someone say –O calligrapher's daughter, and looked up. It was Frei João Álvares. Had the sultan kept his word to his Christian prisoner and allowed her to see the famous manuscript?

To Frei João Álvares's surprise and horror, the young Muslim woman began to weep. What had happened? For a long time she could not speak. At last she said, in a voice so low he had to bend to hear her —He who wants will have nothing, and he who desires nothing will have everything.

—Forgive me, said Frei João Álvares politely, but I'm afraid I don't—

—I wanted to create the world's most beautiful Qur'an. I thought it was to honour Allah, but now I see it was to gain acclaim for my talents. Now I have witnessed a Qur'an that surpasses anything I will ever be capable of.

—May I? said Frei João Álvares, and sat down beside her on the bench, taking care not to touch her kaftan. —If you will permit me, I should like to tell you a story.

The young woman gulped back her sobs and nodded.

—Once upon a time, many years ago, there was a young man of my own order, a Knight of St. Benedict, who dedicated his life to producing illuminated copies of the Bible.

Frei João Álvares noticed that the young woman seemed to stiffen, but he went on.

—The young man became known for his skill and his holiness, and in time, when he was no longer so young, a new king was crowned who asked him to be his personal chaplain. Soon afterwards, the new chaplain visited the king's libraries and came across a magnificent Bible produced by a group of monks in a distant Irish monastery. The chaplain was overwhelmed. He went to the king and told him he could no longer serve him. When the king asked why, the chaplain said, *Because I have discovered a group of monks who are so enlightened that it is as if the Bible they produced is on fire. I must seek them out so I may learn from them.* The king, as you can imagine, was most displeased, and told his chaplain that he could not refuse a royal appointment. *On the contrary, your majesty,* the chaplain said, *I have been ordered to serve a yet greater majesty than your own, and that is a summons I dare not disobey.* The king wanted to throw him into the deepest dungeon, and it was only the intervention of the master of my order that at last persuaded him otherwise. As for the chaplain, he left Portugal for Ireland that very day and was never seen again in his native land.

There was silence for a long while, except for an occasional sob from the calligrapher's daughter. At last she said, wiping her eyes with her veil — which by now was rather soggy —Why did you tell me this story?

—Because you are like that chaplain. Worldly honours do not satisfy you. It is to the dissatisfied that God — Allah, as you know Him — calls. Perhaps He is calling you.

There was another long silence. At last Frei João Álvares said —You are perhaps thinking that it is impertinent of me to compare you to a Christian?

—No, the calligrapher's daughter said. —*I* do not matter. But to compare the revelation of the Qur'an, dictated by the Angel Jibra'il himself to Muhammad...

—The Angel Gabriel also revealed the forthcoming birth of Jesus to Mary, Frei João Álvares said. —And your faith accepts Jesus as one of the Messengers of God, does it not?

The calligrapher's daughter nodded, with some irritation. Who was this Christian to be lecturing her about the tenets of her faith?

—Perhaps, said Frei João Álvares, we are all sons and daughters of the same God, whatever name we know Him by.

—Why, said the calligrapher's daughter wonderingly, are you not angry with us? You fought for your faith against us, and you lost. Why are you not filled with hate?

Frei João Álvares paused, as if considering his words. —Five years provides much time in which to ponder. During that time I have learned Arabic and talked with learned men. The sultan's personal physician is a Jew. One of his most trusted advisers is a Christian. And the holiest man at court may be the slave who feeds the sultan's peacocks. Under the skin all blood is red, is it not?

In the morning, after her prayers, the calligrapher's daughter asked for directions to the peacocks' enclosure. She watched as an elderly black slave unfastened the gate and entered, carrying a bucket of grain. The peahens and their chicks came scurrying, while the male followed more slowly, spreading his lordly tail. It shimmered in the sunlight, an iridescent fan of green and blue and gold that changed from moment to moment. Like a living page torn from the Hidden Book, the calligrapher's daughter thought. Nothing, not even the Qur'an she had seen in the sultan's library, could begin to compare with such an infinity of hues and tones and colours. The slave swept out an arm, scattering the grain, and the chicks and hens bobbed and wove and scuffled with each other in pursuit of the food.

When the bucket was empty, the slave took some chopped-up fruit from a pouch at his belt and knelt. At once the birds began pecking it out of his hands. Several of the peahens nibbled his ear or pecked at his hair, as if he were one of them. After the fruit was gone they still lingered, while the chicks darted in and out between his legs. One or two of the hens allowed him to caress them, as if they were some strange family, peafowl and human. A verse from a surah from the Qur'an — Surat Al-'An'ām, "The

Cattle"—came to the mind of the calligrapher's daughter: *There is not an animal that lives on the earth, nor a flying creature on two wings, but forms part of communities like you.*

At last the slave rose, picked up the empty bucket, and passed again through the gate, fastening it behind him. The calligrapher's daughter hurried over to him. What must it be like, to be in the presence of a page written by Allah Himself? She blurted out her question, but the slave, instead of speaking, opened his mouth and pointed inside.

He had no tongue.

The calligrapher's daughter was horrified. Had he been deliberately mutilated when he was captured? Then how had he and the Christian friar conversed? The slave bowed low, turned, and disappeared into the servants' quarters of the palace. The calligrapher's daughter watched him go and then knelt in the dust beside the enclosure, her fingers gripping the palisades.

That evening the calligrapher's daughter wrote a letter to the sultan. This time the pen flowed like breath across the paper, and each letter seemed to rise up of its own accord. *Your majesty*, the calligrapher's daughter wrote, *I have the answer you sought to your question. Look to your slave, the one who feeds the royal peacocks. For did not the Prophet, peace be upon him, say,* All creatures are the family of Allah, and He loves the most those who are the most beneficent to His family? *Compared to this slave, all the Qur'ans in the world pale into insignificance, including mine. Therefore, your majesty, I beseech you to allow me to return to my home and my family, where I will practise my art with the humility I have learned.*

It is not recorded whether the request of the calligrapher's daughter was granted by the sultan, nor whether Frei João Álvares ever returned to his own country. But it is known that many more Qur'ans flowed from her pen, and each of them glowed with such fire that a new name was bestowed upon her — the Illumined One.

THE MASTER OF SALT

They were white-robed, the monks, and they worked the white salt on the green island bordered by the white foam of the Atlantic. That was how Brother Gérard knew their toils were holy and divinely ordered, and how blessed he was to find himself among them, even though he himself was a lay brother only and his robe matched the dark earth under his sandals. He served the white crystals that lay gleaming in the salt pans under the summer sun, and the crystals in turn served the white monks, who foreswore salt themselves but sold it to the noble houses of Europe so that it might sustain the monastery. The abbot himself had explained to Brother Gérard how the white of the salt matched the white of the lily that was said to have bloomed in the Virgin's hands as a foretelling of the Christ Child to come.

Brother Gérard tried to remember this on those days of heavy rain when the dykes turned to mud and he sank, slowly, toward hell. Also on winter days when he raked the bottom of the pans clean, spattering himself with clay. Mud and clay were also holy, as creations of the Lord, and as necessary to the flourishing of the salt as the sun was, though Brother Gérard couldn't help regretting the Lord's choice of materials on the days when he was knee-deep in the stuff. Such criticism of the divine order led him to confession, where on muddy knees, cold and trembling, he acknowledged yet again his sin of foolish thought and his offence against Holy Scripture. Brother Firmín, who came from Andalusia, said loudly and often—though never in the hearing of the abbot—that he didn't see why the Heavenly Father, *¡Dios me perdone!*, couldn't have situated the salt in some more agreeable climate where they might bake their bones after a day's work.

Brother Gérard had come to the monastery as a boy of twelve, soon after Abbot Isaac had taken up his post on this tiny island ten miles from the shores of France. Banished, so people said, from the abbey of Stella near the city of Poitiers because of a dispute with his superiors. On the contrary, said others, he had chosen isolation in order to expunge some unnamed sin through hard work and privation. From stars to salt, in any event—or mud, depending on how you looked at it. What was not in question was that Abbot Isaac believed in hard work and drove no one harder than himself. A strange man, Abbot Isaac. First of all was the fact of his being from the strange land of England, though admittedly he had studied in Paris and become a white monk at the mother house of Cîteaux. He spoke a pinched adenoidal Latin, quite incomprehensible to the lay brothers, but when agitated reverted to his native tongue. In this language, apparently, it was acceptable to curse the Lord (according to Brother Marrec, who had been a Breton fisherman before joining the order and knew a little English). When the abbot of Cluny informed Abbot Isaac that it was improper for tonsured monks to begrime their hands and their habits with rustic labours, Abbot Isaac shouted (though whether as salutation or profanity no one knew) –Christ! Christ Himself was not above dirtying his hands in order to save us! Christ Himself is the Gardener of our souls! Have you no humility?

The boy Gérard was apprenticed to the abbey's lay brothers as a *saunier*, a salt worker. From Brother Michel and Brother Hervé and Brother Clément he learned how to draw the seawater through the narrow canals into the evaporating basins, and then through even narrower channels into the shallowest basins of all, where the summer sun dried the salt. He learned that a storm with heavy rain might damage the salt crop with too much fresh water, while too much sun would dry out the crystals and render them unusable. He learned the use of the *rouable* for removing the soft mud and algae from the bottom of the salt pans in winter, and the *simoussi* for raking the coarse grey salt from the pans in summer. But it was ten years before he was allowed to touch the *souvron*, the long-handled trapezoidal board used by the master sauniers for lifting the pure top layer, the delicate pinkish-white *fleur de sel* that smelled like violets. Of the half-dozen master sauniers he was most in awe of Brother Thibault, himself a white monk and the abbey's choirmaster. Brother Thibault was old and thin and stooped, yet no one produced better saltflower, and it was said that he sang to his salt to produce its glistening crystals.

Gérard cautiously tried this himself when no one was looking, inexperienced though he still was with the souvron. Alas, his singing had no such effect. He was only a lay brother, after all, a peasant boy from his tiny village a mile or two from the abbey. Like the other brothers he sang behind the high screen that separated them, in church as in life, from the white monks — separate refectories and dormitories, separate passages and hallways, even separate latrines. Only at harvest, when all hands were needed in the salt pans to gather in the crop, did he mingle with them.

—You look tired, *mon fils*, his mother said one October evening. It was a grey day, colder and rainier than usual, and he'd almost fallen asleep over his soup. At fourteen he still went home every day, as he would until he made his vows, if he chose, at eighteen. Perhaps, though, he wasn't fitted? The cellarer, Brother Albéric, had spoken harshly to him that afternoon when he'd stumbled and a section of dyke wall had fallen away. Afterwards, rebuilding the wall, he shed unmanly tears, for which he chastised himself. He would pray to the familiar blue statue of Our Lady in his own parish church, whose own son, after all, must sometimes have spilt the nails in his father's carpentry shop.

—Don't send Jean-Marie to the salt, he said suddenly. Jean-Marie, twelve next month, was to join him in the salt pans, which had supported them all since their father's death from the scrofula. But Jean-Marie was a frail boy; he wouldn't flourish. —Find something else for him to do. Please, Maman.

—Your sister's been offered a place at the seigneur's when she turns eleven, his mother said, bringing him a mug of warmed cider. Another year, then; Élisabeth had just turned ten. One less mouth to feed. Then there would only be the two youngest, Mathieu and Anne, at home.

He himself was already promised; that he understood. First as the family's breadwinner, and second as their offering to God, their amulet against further illness or loss. Or rather, God Himself had chosen him for this humble task and had provided this means of sustenance. He could have been sent to the abbey's pigsty, the brewery, the granary; instead, in the summer breezes, he was surrounded by the smell of violets, that humble three-leaved flower of the trinity that the Virgin herself had loved.

At fifteen, unexpectedly, he fell in love. The girl, a neighbour's daughter with a long brown plait and a toss of freckles across her nose, turned suddenly, at fourteen, into a woman. She pretended not to notice him anymore, crossing her father's yard with the milk pail, but one evening she followed him down to the shore where he stood among the rock pools watching the stints and sanderlings. A few evenings later, when he asked, she went with him. He told her of his feelings and she dipped her chin, which he took as a yes. A few months later she was affianced to the son of the wealthiest farmer in the district.

Again he wept unmanly tears into his pillow. The rejection was a call to vocation, a reminder about his future. He would not marry. He would hold his future nieces and nephews on his knee, on those rare feast days when he was permitted visits home, but otherwise he belonged to the Church.

At eighteen he became a novice, learning by heart the four prayers that the brothers recited in silence during their labours: the Lord's Prayer, the Creed, the Miserere, the Ave Maria. He slept now in the dormitory, in the narrow bed that would be his for the rest of his life. A year later, in the abbey's chapel, he made his vows in front of all the monks, white and brown. He was grateful, when his mother died nine months afterwards, that she had lived to witness his commitment to God. At her funeral the knot of villagers outside the parish church parted to let him through, a tall bearded young man in a frayed brown robe.

But the proudest moment of his life came when he was chosen, three years after his vows, to be apprenticed to Brother Thibault himself. No lay brother had ever been apprenticed to a white monk before. Brother Thibault was crumbling like the salt itself, yet he refused to leave his saltflower. If God permitted, he told Gérard, he would die in the salt pans with the smell of the *fleur de sel* in his nostrils. Meanwhile he would teach the raw young peasant with the flair for the souvron how to rely on smell and texture alone to determine the quality, since none of the monks had so much as tasted the crop for which they were famous.

It was a year or two later when Brother Thibault whispered to Gérard the secret of his salt. He had, apparently, received unearthly assistance. One summer, many years before, the Virgin herself had visited him, wrapped in her blue cloak, her face obscured by radiance. He'd been young then, not much older than Gérard. She had moved toward him along the dykes, her feet barely touching the ground, her hands lifted in benediction. Overcome by terror and incredulity, he told no one. The following summer she came again, this time with her mother, the blessed St. Anne, and wiped his brow with her sleeve. He must have fainted, because he came to with his fellow monks standing over him, urging him to rise. Publicly, he blamed the fainting spell on the heat, but ever since, his salt had been the whitest and most perfumed in the region. The king himself was rumoured to insist on Brother Thibault's salt at his table, and the small pottery jars that bore Brother Thibault's signature were said to fetch extraordinary prices in Genoa and Saxony.

These stories brought their own terrors to Brother Gérard. How, once Brother Thibault had departed this earthly life, was he to maintain the quality of the crop? If the salt's unique characteristics depended on heavenly assistance, how was he, a mere lay brother, to obtain it? He redoubled the fervency and frequency of his prayers. A visit from Our Lady would be at a time and place not of his choosing, but he made it plain that, if she should deign to honour him in such a way, he would keep her statue in the parish church permanently lit with candles. He would also — how, he didn't know — make a pilgrimage to the cathedral dedicated to her in Paris, and would undertake any other arduous practices she might require. When his sister Élisabeth, now married, bore a daughter, he wrote to ask if she would name the child Violette, after the Virgin's favourite flower.

At the monastery, time stood still. Or rather, time moved in a circle under the dome of heaven, through the round of the year. For Brother Gérard, time moved through the seasons of the salt, marked by more or less mud, more or less rain or sun or wind. One year a heavy snowfall, never before seen in the region, meant they could not clean the pans in time for spring, and the salt crop was much reduced. Another year a fire destroyed many of the barns and outbuildings, and Brother Gérard found himself working with the carpenters and other lay brothers, under the supervision of Brother Albéric, in the rebuilding. The abbot had decreed this reassignment of duties as a mortification, on the grounds that the monks must have so displeased the Lord that He had sent a fire to consume part of their possessions. Something to do with the hotter passions, such as lust or anger, the abbot implied. Brother Gérard went twice to confession that week, remembering how he had glanced longingly at a woman walking past on the road from the village, and how he had raised his voice impatiently with Brother Clotaire, a man as strong and dimwitted as an ox.

It did not occur to him to question the idea of communal guilt. Once, the bread being made a little less coarse than usual, the abbot placed the whole community under penance to atone for the fault of the baker.

Word came, from a pair of mendicant monks, that a force of thirteen thousand troops on their way to the crusades had helped the Portuguese army to drive the Moors out of Lisbon. Many in the abbey fell to their knees and gave thanks to God for rescuing a Christian kingdom from the infidels. But Abbot Isaac, that Sunday, gave a sermon not merely strange, but — to some at least — diabolical. He spoke against the forcing of unbelievers to embrace Christian beliefs at the point of a sword, and of the lack of Christian martyrdom for those who killed and pillaged. What belief could occur under such circumstances? Would Christ Himself, given his gentleness and patience, have behaved in such a manner? And why, then, should the enemy not say –Do to the church as the church has done?

The sermon prompted fierce and whispered arguments throughout the abbey. How then, Brother Lucien wanted to know, did one do battle against the enemies of the Church?

The pope himself, after all, had called for the crusade. The kings of France and Germany had assembled their armies. Had the abbot gone mad? Two of the kitchen monks, Brother Louis and Brother Antoine, came almost to blows, but were separated by Brother Thomas with the aid of a large kitchen knife. Brother Lucas — a fellow countryman of Abbot Isaac — said the fact that it had been raining since the news came showed that heaven itself and all its inhabitants were weeping. Brother Firmín, banging a fist on the refectory table, said the sooner the infidels were driven from his own country the better, whether by sword or sorcery or a scattering of salt to ward off the devil. Brother Gérard thought, but did not say, that the scent of the monastery salt alone would induce the bravest infidel to lay down his weapons and accept the Saviour on the spot.

It was, perhaps, not unforeseen that Abbot Isaac would be accused of heresy. At the famous abbey of Clairvaux, Abbot Bernard was known to champion those knights of Christ who had joined the crusade. He had been sent to preach to the king and queen of France by the pope himself, and all the princes and lords had thrown themselves at his feet to receive the pilgrims' cross. In Germany, where he had also preached, it was said he had cured the blind, the lame, a girl with a withered hand. —Christ is risen! the crowds had shouted, weeping, jubilant, as the bells rang. When Bernard knelt at the statue of the Virgin in the royal chapel in Speyer, white roses had bloomed at her feet.

Brother Thibault, at work in the salt pans, said —Would to God I had been taken before these horrors were visited upon us. Gérard stared at him, dumbstruck, but it turned out that he wasn't speaking, at least at first, of Bernard. Brother Thibault waved the souvron dangerously. —Are we pagans ourselves that we must murder and defile? Did the Lord do such things? No, he did not. Brother Thibault flung the souvron into the nearest salt pan, where it slowly sank from view. –How the body of Christ has gone astray, all for a few cheap miracles!

In bed that night, Gérard lay awake, probing cautiously at what Brother Thibault had said. It was blasphemy, of course, to accuse the Church of having lost its way. Yet, given the choice, Gérard would have sided with Brother Thibault. He was too fearful to say so in public, but if called upon he would defend Brother Thibault to the death. Brother Thibault, after all, had divine dispensation for his salt-gathering, which wounded no one and sanctified all.

The following day Brother Thibault disappeared. Some said he had retreated to a hermitage in the Ardennes forest, others that he had discarded the habit and returned to his native Auvergne. Whatever the case, he would not have abandoned his crop in the middle of the season if he had any intention of returning. Gérard, to his horror, was placed in charge of the miraculous salt pans.

Desperate times called for desperate measures. Gérard began singing to the salt again. He hummed under his breath if any of the other brothers were nearby, but otherwise kept up a steady stream of hymns and chants. After a week or two, tiring of the repetition, he added the old folk songs his mother had sung in his childhood. Cautiously, one at a time, because it might be another kind of blasphemy to sing profane songs over the blessed salt. When nothing divine nor satanic happened, he added another, and then another. When he ran out he turned to the bawdy songs he and the other boys had sung as they drove the cows home or went hunting birds with their slingshots. Given that the Lord had designed human beings to desire the opposite sex, it might be supposed that He wouldn't mind the odd risqué verse or two. Better a lusty chorus than the pious quaverings of some of the more hypocritical villagers.

He woke, that week, to an odd glow shining through the open window. It seemed to come from the salt pans. He dressed and ran outside. The moon was full, and all its light seemed concentrated on the salt, as if the moon were vying with the sun for the ripening of it. But then the moon went behind a cloud and the light from the salt faded. Gérard went back to his bed abashed. Miracles did not come to those whose mouths hung open waiting for them. He knelt by his bed and prayed for forgiveness, and promised the Lord there would be no more resorting to the secular in his singing.

He had his sister bring his niece, Violette, to the abbey and took her walking along the dykes. She was a quiet, bright-eyed, obedient child, whose innocence would be pleasing to the Virgin, and whose name might add perfume to the salt. After the workday was done he took to sitting dreamily by the pans, imagining angels descending, using their wings to fan the salt. He was certain, once or twice, that their wings had brushed him, and once he found a long white feather—too long, he thought, to be from any bird.

Abbot Isaac, most unusually, came to see how he was getting on. Brother Albéric had told him that Gérard was the most devoted worker in the monastery, especially since the loss of Brother Thibault. To crucify oneself in the service of Christ, Abbot Isaac said approvingly, was most admirable. Brother Gérard was a model even the white monks might emulate. Gérard thought of his lusty singing, his attempts to induce miracles, and told the abbot that his thoughts outstripped his attempts to mortify the body.

–Indeed, said the abbot, all of us find ourselves in that position. Even the saintly Bernard, I suspect. I am sure the Lord will favour you in the salt production, as he did Brother Thibault.

But the salt, at the end of that summer, was definitely inferior. It was true that an unusual hailstorm had done a great deal of damage, but perhaps that was the Lord's answer to the lusty songs? Whatever the reason, Gérard crumbled the salt flakes between his fingers, noting the lack of lustre, the absence of scent. The other salt masters had done no better, but that was no consolation. He, Brother Gérard, was a fraud. Brother Thibault had taught him well, but he could not pass on the divine favour he had been granted.

After the failure of the salt, Abbot Isaac was summoned to the motherhouse at Cîteaux. The failure was proof, if one were needed, that the abbot had incurred divine displeasure, which had no doubt begun with that notorious sermon in which he had denied Christian martyrdom to those who went into battle for the Lord. It was known that the abbot at Cîteaux was much influenced by Bernard.

Gérard watched him go, sitting astride his elderly horse, followed by two of the white monks on foot. Would Abbot Isaac be recalled, and replaced by someone more congenial to Bernard and his followers? Would he disappear, as Brother Thibault had?

Gérard spent the day on his knees in the chapel. It had been raining heavily for a week, turning the fields into lakes and the salt pans into lagoons that overflowed the dykes. He asked for nothing; instead, swaying a little as the day drew on, he listened. Perhaps, busy with his requests, not to mention his singing, he had drowned out the Lord. Perhaps, instead of a visit from the Virgin and St. Anne, the Lord was providing other sorts of instruction instead, some of which might concern the salt. At the end of the day he rose, stiffly, to his feet, made the sign of the cross, and bowed his head. The sanctuary lamp in its niche flickered and went out. Gérard paid no attention. This time he would not be fooled. He would be patient and obedient. He would expect nothing.

The basins were unworkable while the rain continued, so Gérard lent a hand where needed, in the dormitories, the scriptorium, the stables. He chose the lowliest tasks, the most disagreeable chores. He listened to the scratch of the monks' pens as he sharpened their nibs, the soft murmurings of the cows when he shovelled dung, the white monks practising their chants below him while, above, he emptied the night's chamber pots into a pail. He would not go back to the salt. What he would do instead he did not yet know, but the answer would come in time. He spoke to no one and did not even pray under his breath while working lest he miss some divine word, some sign, some admonition.

Abbot Isaac returned just before the celebration of the Nativity. It was a bitter winter that year, colder than anything anyone remembered, and when they helped the abbot off his horse, it was said that his habit was frozen stiff. Shortly after, he came down with the lung-fever, and when neither spiced wine nor bleeding nor purgation did any good, Gérard slipped out of the abbey and went to the house of old Mathilde, who had been the midwife and healer in his village since his childhood and had once cured his little sister Anne of epilepsy. Mathilde, promised a daily mass for her soul in the abbey itself when she died, gave him a folded bit of cloth containing a powder that was to be added to warmed milk taken fresh from the cow. Gérard managed to be in the barn the following morning at milking time and stole a cup from the bucket when Brother Josselin was busy elsewhere. He took the warmed milk himself to the foot of the staircase that led to the abbot's bedroom, and begged the monk in charge, Brother Gregorius, to see that the abbot drank it. The purity of the milk, he explained, would remove whatever impurities had sickened the abbot. Brother Gregorius, who came from the kingdom of Poland, was old and superstitious — not really a Christian at all, it was sometimes murmured. He took the cup carefully in his hands and told Gérard, in his rich Polish accent, that such a holy offering could only do the abbot good.

Abbot Isaac's ill health continued into the new year, though all the monks, white and brown, said a special prayer on Christ's Mass and for the eleven days thereafter. Brother Firmín said, darkly, that it seemed importunate to burden a newborn babe with the weight of their abbot's illness, on his birthday no less, but Brother Clotaire — he of the dim wits — astonished everyone by answering, slowly but firmly, that a baby who had been reborn annually for the last thousand years was unlikely to find anything importunate or, for that matter, surprising. Gérard, at Compline that evening, found himself thinking of the cup of warmed milk, and of the cow that had provided it, and of Mary herself in the stablelight, nursing the babe with the warmth of the beasts upon her.

Abbot Isaac recovered, after a fashion, but was too weak to perform many of his former duties. After some months during which several squabbles broke out and Brother Ignatius accused Brother Florent of stealing the missal his mother had given him — which he should not have been so attached to in the first place, as Brother Lucas observed tartly — a new abbot was appointed. He arrived, preceded by many rumours, on a day in spring when most of the brothers were out of doors, in the fields and the orchard and the vegetable garden. Gérard, helping to prune the pear trees, watched in amazement as a tall young man on a white horse cantered through the abbey gates. He swung himself down with one hand on the pommel, a vivid purple cloak with scarlet lining swirling about him. He might have been a king or an emperor rather than a monk.

The cloak, he explained to them that evening at dinner, had been a gift from Abbot Bernard, who had had it from the pope himself. He intended to sell it and use the funds for the abbey. Kyril was his name, and this was his first posting as abbot. He was Greek by birth but had been raised in Italy and then France. He laughed, to their horror; he drank wine, he told charming stories. He was like a princeling, good-looking, dazzlingly erudite. No wonder Bernard was so impressed, though *smitten* was the word Brother Firmín used. *Enamorado*, he added, under his breath so that no one heard.

And yet, and yet... Along with the charm and boyish-ness came firmness, calm, impartiality. He sat beside Abbot Isaac at the evening meal and deferred to him on matters of doctrine. As Abbot Isaac had done, he visited those monks who were sick, and from time to time sent his monks to the villages, to see who might be in need of their produce or their ministrations. The cloak, so it was said, brought in seventy-five livres. A portion was sent to Rome; the remainder was used to buy beeswax candles, new robes, a cushion for Brother Hervé's bony knees, extra blankets. Even Abbot Isaac, who had trouble sleeping, was given a larger room, strewn with fresh hay and lavender each morning, though Gérard was certain he wouldn't have approved. What had happened to their mortifications? As if able to hear thoughts, Abbot Kyril preached on that very subject the following Sunday. Mortification was, he said, like any spiritual practice, capable of being abused. It did no good if it rendered men incapable of carrying out their duties, becoming then a burden on others. Gérard wondered if this was a reference to Abbot Isaac, who had insisted on travelling home in his thinnest robe, having given his thicker one away. Or perhaps his illness was an affliction from God for the abbot's heresy?

Another admission came, this time from Brother Gregorius. —I confess, he told Gérard, looking troubled, that I failed to give that cup of milk to Abbot Isaac that morning. The monk in charge of the infirmary had forbidden it. Milk was known to increase mucus, and who knew what it might do to Abbot Isaac's recovery, however well-meant? —So I drank it myself, Brother Gregorius said. —But I wanted you to know the good it did after all. It cured my arthritis.

In October, after the harvest was in, Abbot Kyril summoned Gérard to his office. Why was he no longer serving the salt, as he had done since boyhood? Matters had been explained to him, but he hadn't understood. Why would one with such a gift, of such importance to the abbey—not to mention God—turn away from it?

Gérard explained, as best he could under the abbot's inquiring gaze, what had happened. —Yes, yes, Kyril said impatiently. —I've been informed of all this. And of the unfortunate departure of Brother Thibault. But one failure of the salt crop, and that likely due to a hailstorm...

—Brother Thibault had no such failures, Gérard said softly.

—Not of the salt, perhaps, Kyril said. —But no man succeeds in everything. Our Lord sends mistakes that we might learn from them. Not to punish us.

Gérard was about to explain the facts of Brother Thibault's divine favour—though reluctantly, since it might sound like special pleading—when the abbot said abruptly —Have you heard of St. Cyril of Jerusalem? Whose name I took when I became a monk?

Gérard tried to remember the stories of saints from his parish boyhood, but drew a blank. Cyril, apparently, had either done nothing memorable or failed to come to a gory end.

—He sold a robe of gold thread, given by the Emperor Constantine to the bishop, to keep his people from starving, Kyril said quietly. —Because of that he was sent into exile. I have always found him a most admirable model.

Lacking any such robe, or anything else, to sell, Gérard looked puzzled. Kyril smiled. —I mention him because of his belief in forgiveness. He forgave those who exiled him. *The Spirit comes gently and makes himself known by his fragrance*, he wrote. *The Spirit is not felt as a burden, for God is light, very light.* Kyril looked intently at Gérard, as though listening to something. —Perhaps you have been seeking guidance in the wrong places. Through sight, for example, or hearing. But as St. Cyril suggests, God may also be known through his fragrance, no? And where better to meet that fragrance but through the salt? Did not Jesus exhort us to be not only the light of the world but also the salt of the earth? You, Brother Gérard, have a special calling. You are to be the dispenser of salty radiance.

Brother Gérard laughed softly to himself that evening as he shovelled dung in the stables, and the next morning when he emptied the chamber pots in the dormitories. Dung and urine also had fragrance, though perhaps not radiance. Perhaps God had been speaking all along and he hadn't noticed, so lowly were the materials he chose. Like the mud in the dykes and the algae in the salt pans. Perhaps he was guilty, not of wanting to honour his teacher but of pride, of wanting his salt to be better than anyone else's. He had forgotten, after all, that the body itself exuded salt, in its sweat and tears; from birth to death, humankind was bathed in the substance.

The following Sunday Abbot Kyril preached another sermon. —Abbot Isaac spoke to you of mercy, said Kyril, as Abbot Isaac, wrapped in his new blanket, nodded from the front row, and I speak to you of forgiveness. *Be seasoned, then, with God's salt, so that the mind that is drenched and weakened by the waves of this world is held steady.*

Gérard would have sworn that Abbot Kyril was looking directly at him as he spoke, except that such a fancy smacked of pride again. Certainly he had been seasoned; certainly he had been drenched and held steady. Of such muddy and wayward journeys was life made. He would dig Brother Thibault's souvron out of the salt pan. He would clean the mud off, revelling in the smell of earth and rain and rot, and begin again.

THE OLD SPEECH

The house stood at the end of the lane. The old man had his own way of talking.

—Claistered and clackhammered he was! Harkelled and wyethotted! Aye, he was that, and no's the brab'll say otherwise!

The child's mother set her down with a toy while she put the old man's supper to heat. He told stories that no one understood. Sometimes he laughed to himself, softly. It was a pity, folks said, that he had the Speech, now that no one else thereabouts knew it. His wife had been the last one who did, and she'd died years before. There was a son somewhere, so rumour had it, but if there was he never visited. He'd be off in the city, living his own life, forgetting the Speech entirely.

The child seemed to understand, though. Sometimes she dropped her toy and watched the old man, fingers in her mouth. Once or twice she'd said some word or other that came from him, or so the mother thought. But if she did, the old man didn't notice. He lived, mostly, in some other world where people understood him.

The child's mother had no time to spend deciphering his tongue. She'd arrived the year before, pregnant, her husband picked up in one of the Cleansings, perhaps; at any rate he'd gone out one day and never come home. She didn't look for him. It was better not to ask. In the town they assigned her to the old man and paid her to look after him. She was given the garage next door, cleaned out, serviceable enough. When the child came she named her Lina.

—Lina! the old man said, and drew a shaky picture of a flower with wide petals, which she understood to be a plant known by that name on the island he came from.

The island itself was unnameable, for the name, like so much else, had gone.

Two people came from the university to record the old man. *Smetherin,* they called the Speech, though no one in the town had heard that name. Even the old man, said to be one of the last few fluent speakers, mixed his words with English, and parts of the grammar had gone forever. Still, it was important to collect what was left.

But what was the point? Lina's mother thought. Like collecting the bones of some ancient animal. Sad, to be sure, but in the midst of all the other sadnesses, not terribly important. The old man would die soon, and there would be an end of it.

Smetherin. Also Smeathrin, Smederin, Smedren. Currently found only on two or three of the Outer Islands. Fluent speakers worldwide: fewer than 12. With no formal orthography, it is not being passed on to a new generation and no extant oral histories remain. Classified as an erratic as it has been little studied or attested. Believed to be composed of old Greenlandic verb forms and Old Norse nouns, with Latin terms a later addition when the islands were Christianized in the tenth century. A counting rhyme remains: smetch, vetch, taddle, treddle, cinqueme, sisset, soryvet, oitch. The numeric system is based on a unit of 8, with numbers repeated for higher figures.

—Soryvet, oitch, the old man said, and then louder —Soryvet! Oitch!

How was she supposed to know what he meant?

—Soryvet, the little girl said. —Pee-pee. Now how had she learned that? The old man motioned. Sure enough, he wanted the chamber pot, and an oitch followed the soryvet into the bowl. —Oitch! Lina shrieked, delighted. —Oitch!

—No, the mother said firmly. —Pee-pee. Poo-poo. But the child covered her face with her fingers and peeked out. —Soryvet! Oitch!

The mother thought perhaps she should look for another job. But they were nearly impossible to find, and this one came with accommodation, however modest. She began leaving Lina with the woman down the street who had two youngsters of her own, paying her in the pies and bread she baked at the old man's house.

—Soryvet! the three children shrieked, playing together. —Oitch!

The woman down the street said she didn't know what her children were learning, but she didn't like it, and perhaps it would be better if Lina didn't come after all.

The mother tried tying Lina to the leg of the table while she worked in the kitchen, but the child cried and howled and the old man, upstairs, banged on the floor with his cane. There was an old dog crate in the back yard, crusted with droppings, that the mother cleaned out and lined with a blanket. Sat in the crate with a toy, Lina was quiet, at least for a while, though sooner or later the howling started again.

–Would a dog help? asked the farmer's boy who came by with the milk. An old farm dog with misted eyes joined them, useless now for guarding sheep. The dog and Lina curled up in the crate together, murmuring, tangled in sleep. The mother was freed to work for hours.

When summer came the old man insisted on a chisel and a hammer and a wooden stool with an embroidered cover. He sat outside by the low wall and tapped at a brick. A *D* appeared and then an *H*. The final word seemed to be unpronounceable in any language. *DHLPT.* Perhaps it was code for something. Or perhaps the old man was finally losing his mind.

The embroidered cover had been made by his wife, whose name the mother could never quite catch. Her dresses, frosted with dust, still hung upstairs; a hairbrush with painted flowers still sat on a night table. One of the dresses, rose red with panels of real velvet, came from some other existence. Once or twice, late at night, the mother opened the closet at the far end of the hall and slipped it on. On the dance floor of a palace somewhere, she spun round the room to the music of an orchestra, her fingertips resting on the arm of a captain in full dress uniform.

The summer, like all summers now, was hot, unbearable. She tried to persuade the old man to go inside. He often sat staring into the distance, his chisel forgotten. She herself placed a chair on the shaded porch, where she could keep an eye on both the old man and Lina. The child staggered up and down the verandah, barricaded by the dog, who growled when she tried for the stairs. Sometimes she lay on top of the dog and sucked her thumb.

—You! Lina's mother!

It was the woman from down the street. She couldn't pronounce Lina's mother's name and hadn't bothered to learn it.

—I need a pie for a guest tonight. How much?

The mother had baked a pie early that morning while it was still cool, filled with the wild berries that grew along the lanes.

—Ten, she said, though she'd been dreaming of fresh pie and clotted cream all day.

—Ten! the other woman said. —How about five?

—Eight, said the mother.

They settled on seven. —Soryvet, the mother said under her breath.

—Oitch, Lina said unexpectedly as the woman hurried off with the glowing dish.

The mother understood that Lina was telling her not to accept a penny less than the pie was worth.

Smetherin speakers are believed to have devised at least two secret languages, and possibly more. One was for communicating with their sled dogs, though only the odd word has survived: tattni, *what does the night smell of,* and rifpulli, *your ears are as soft as a hare's. Others, however, claim that* tattni *and* rifpulli *were simply directional words for the lead dog, and that certain tall tales were presented as truth. Another secret language was used by the women to share knowledge forbidden to men. Menstruation, for example, was referred to, in rough translation, as* the moon strokes your belly, milking blood. *It was taboo for men or boys to use this word or even to know of its existence. There are early, possibly suspect, reports of a murder on the island of Bryebekka because of the use of this word by a young man who attempted to practise magic with it.*

That summer, the longest anyone had known, the mother made pies every morning and sold them—at the price her daughter had stipulated—every afternoon. The oitch notes, as she thought of them, accumulated in her apron pockets and in a locked metal box in the garage where she and Lina slept. The old man still sat with his chisel, tapping out another word at the corner where two walls met. *Roiveliin.* It took him two weeks.

—What does it mean? the mother asked, bringing him a glass of beer.

He spoke the word out loud, once, twice. Lina, bringing up the rear with the dog, repeated it perfectly. The old man turned and stared at her, face lit up. —*She* understands, he said, and pointed a shaking finger. —A dab thelset, she is, and no mattling about it!

The word had several meanings, apparently. Darkness, for one, and a certain type of rain, a sort of dry mist, that fell only on the island the old man came from. And it was also the name of some sort of sweet cake made with raisins and other things the old man lacked the English words for.

—Roiveliin, he said again that evening when the child's

mother gave him a piece of the pie she'd saved out for the three of them.

—Pie, she said. —Wild berry pie.

—Roiveliin, the old man repeated, and then: —*Sposina*. And after a pause —My wife, said in very clear English. And then he wept.

There was enough money now, as the autumn mists swept over the town, to leave. But where would she go? To look for her husband? She lacked that kind of courage. Was this, then, home? It wasn't what she'd intended all those years ago, scratching out her lessons on a chalk slate, dreaming of the future. What kind of home was made up of an old man, partly senile and no relation to her, and a child whose father had disappeared? And the dog, of course. Also old, also likely senile.

Sometimes she watched them, dog and child, how they might have been made from one skin. If the child cried, the dog always knew what she wanted. When the mail-woman came with the letters, or the farmer's boy with the milk crates, the dog stood up on unsteady legs and tottered forward, baring his teeth. *I am a guard dog, still, despite appearances,* he seemed to be saying. *I guard a child. I place my life between you and her.*

One morning, when the mother rose, the old man was not in his bed. She searched the house and at last hurried outside, raincoat flung on. The mist, thick as cold porridge, made her gasp. There, down by the garden wall, a dark hunched shape.

She ran across the grass, slipping and almost falling, and grabbed the old man by the shoulder. —Are you mad? she shouted, and shook him, hard. He turned slowly, his chisel dripping in his hand.

—Claistered and clackhammered, he said. —Time is thottering away, you see. Claisters us all, does time. I didn't see it soon enough.

He wouldn't move, so she ran back inside and pulled a blanket off his bed. She found an old tarp and asked her neighbour, a lean man with sharp edges, to help her set it up over the old man.

—He'll be dead by evening, the neighbour said, as if it was her fault.

—He won't go inside. Do you want to help carry him?

But the old man put up such a struggle, shouting and flailing his arms—not to mention Lina's howling and the dog's barking—that finally they gave up.

It would be on her own head, she thought as the neighbour stumped off. When she was younger there would have been friends to help, or the police, or an ambulance. But now there were none of those things. She ran back inside and stripped off her wet clothes and took Lina into the tub with her.

When dark fell the door was flung open, startling her. The old man stood there, dripping but satisfied. —Aranbollock, he said in a firm clear voice. —That was today. Aranbollock.

She took his arm, fed him supper, and put him to bed. —Aranbollock, he repeated sleepily. —Returned to me yesterday, all on its own, fancy that. Aranbollock.

She would have to leave, she told herself, washing the dishes. She couldn't be expected to put up with this. If the old man got ill, she wasn't a nurse, she hadn't those skills. Nor—a grim thought—was she an undertaker.

–Oitch, Lina mumbled next door in her sleep.

–Oitch, said the dog, or something that sounded very much like oitch. He lifted his head and looked at the child and put his head down on his paws again.

There were three more words: *cloyben, wyfoggren, miliash*.

They came a week apart, each time on a Wednesday. Those were the mornings she found the old man outside at dawn, hunched on his stool, chipping away. Rain or sun, sleet or fog, he worked into the evening, tapping steadily. There was no more sitting and gazing into the distance.

Of course he couldn't go on this way, not indefinitely.

When it was sunny, the child and the dog went out into the garden and played chase. Or tried to; the dog was game but tired quickly. Afterwards Lina moved to the old man and leaned against his knee. He never pushed her away, just patted her head and kept working. Leaves fell, gold and russet and brown, crumpled like burnt paper. The year was sifting slowly into ash. The mother dried berries or made soup or sat and sewed new clothes for Lina. She knitted gloves for herself and even tore up an old coat to make a jacket for the dog.

That evening—the evening after *miliash*—the old man looked up from his dinner of beans and bread. –My cloyben, he told her, will be like this. And he sketched some sort of design on the table with his finger. When she didn't understand he grew impatient. –My cloyben! he shouted, pushing himself to his feet. He lowered himself to the floor and lay down.

—Cloyben, he said again, and sketched the shape of a box in the air around him.

Ah. *Now* she understood. His coffin.

The next day it was snowing hard, and for once the old man stayed inside. Every now and then he got up and paced a little, back and forth. He wouldn't die yet, he told her. He couldn't. He was needed — no, required. He had to continue.

—You've done what you can, she said. But that was a mistake.

—Have you not seen? His hand shook, pointing outside. —*Dantry*, there on the keystone? He'd done that one first, years ago. It had been difficult, standing on a ladder — he'd almost fallen. *Tackle-torsel* had followed, tapped into the window frame, months after; they always came slowly then. Then *smeached*, chiselled on a bottom corner of the house, just above the grass.

His wife had still been alive then, and she'd remembered words too. —I promised her, he said, still shaking. —I made a promise.

The child's mother sat back and stared at him. In all these months it was only the second time he'd mentioned his wife.

—You loved her very much, she said tentatively.

—Loved her? Nothing to do with love. He groped in the air. —To do with protecting. *Bakkinsleemin*. That is what our words are. They use us for protection.

∅

That evening they sat, the snow still falling outside, and listened, she and the child. It was difficult, getting her tongue around the words, but Lina said each one as if she already knew it. The dog listened too, giving nothing away. The dog regularly licked the words on the walls, knowing each by its feel and taste and smell. They were pale things compared to the rest of the world, but the child had touched each of them, following the old man round the garden, and that was enough.

Fire Breathing: The words attributed to the First Nations firekeeper are taken from an interview by Yvette Brend of CBC News British Columbia with Pierre Kruger, an Elder with the Penticton Indian Band, speaking about his late mother, Annie Kruger, a traditional firekeeper on what is now called Syilx territory.

The Master of Salt: Abbot Kyril's final prayer borrows from John the Deacon's sixth-century Letter to Senarius.

ACKNOWLEDGEMENTS AND THANKS

I'd like to thank the editors of the following journals and anthologies in which versions of some of these stories first appeared: *The New Quarterly*, *Prairie Fire*, *Dark Mountain 9* (UK), *Image Journal* (US), *Tesseracts Seventeen*, and *Best Canadian Stories 2013*.

My grateful thanks to the Canada Council for the Arts, the Manitoba Arts Council, and the Arts Section of Yukon Tourism and Culture through Lotteries Yukon for financial support of this work. I'm particularly grateful to the Writers' Trust for giving me a grant in 2018. A special thank you to my siblings, Andrew, Duncan, and Kerry, and their spouses for generosity above and beyond, as well as to Eve D'Aeth, Kari Hipwell, and Lise Friisbaastad.

I've been sustained throughout by writer friends, especially Sharon English—twin soul—and by the crucial work of the Dark Mountain Project in the UK.

Writing residencies at Green College, University of BC, Vancouver; the Haig-Brown House in Campbell River, BC; the Kingston Frontenac Public Library in Kingston, ON; and the Millennium Library in Winnipeg, MB, provided income and writing time. My gratitude to Mark Vessey, Sandra Parrish, Kimberly Sutherland-Mills, Danielle Pilon, and their staffs, who were invariably welcoming and supportive. To all the participants I met in workshops and one-on-one, you taught me more than you know. A big high-five to the Kingston Teen Fantasy group, who knew to their bones how essential other dimensions are.

Working with the stellar crew at Goose Lane Editions has been a revelation. A deep bow to my editor, Bethany Gibson, for her insight and tact; to Peter Norman, copy editor *par excellence*; and to Julie Scriver for managing to channel the entire book in her cover design.

To Erling, first reader, whose faith never wavered even when mine did, and to our boreal husky Freya (2006–19), extraordinary canine companion and teacher: my deepest gratitude for your love and belief, always.

The Yukon, where I lived for twenty years, has never left me. Raven, Willow Herb, and Tágà Shäw (Great River) are on every page.

Born in the UK, Patricia Robertson grew up in British Columbia and received her MA in Creative Writing from Boston University. Her first collection of short stories, *City of Orphans*, was shortlisted for the Ethel Wilson Fiction Prize, while her second collection, *The Goldfish Dancer*, was hailed by the *National Post* as "a work of insight and mastery." She was awarded the Aesthetica International Prize for Poetry in 2018.

Robertson's fiction and essays have appeared in *Best Canadian Stories* and *Best Canadian Essays* and have been shortlisted for the Journey Prize, the CBC Literary Awards, the Pushcart Prize, and the National Magazine Awards. She has served as writer-in-residence at libraries and universities across Canada and currently lives in Winnipeg, located on Treaty 1 territory, the traditional territory of Anishinaabeg, Cree, Oji-Cree, Dakota, and Dene Peoples, and the homeland of the Métis Nation.